# The Wife, the Mistress, and the Guinea Pig

### & Other Stories

## Isle of Arran u3a Creative Writing Group

# Dedication

*Take a disparate group of casual scribblers, join them together to creatively write, and they wander in a world of words. Memoir, fiction, poetry — there is no limit to ambition — encouraged, guided, sometimes gently criticised by our mentor and other members. Feeding off each other's ideas and enthusiasm, this anthology is our baby, child of many parents to whom it is dedicated.*

Bear me o'er the seas to Arran,
To the Isle I love so well;
There my thoughts are ever straying,
And tis there I long to dwell.

*Giù lain mile beannachd bhuamsa*
*Null gu eil - ean*
*Far an tric an toir mo bhruadar*
*Mi air chuairt thar chluaintean gaoil.*

— WORDS AND MUSIC BY ANGUS KENNEDY, GAELIC BY
FINLAY J. MACDONALD

# Foreword

Tapping into the expertise and experience of those who were no longer in full-time careers, the UK-based University of the Third Age was founded in 1982 on the theory that we learn most by doing and learn best from each other. Today the u3a includes 1,035 chapters with nearly 400,000 members.

The u3a chapter on Arran sprung into life in the autumn of 2019 with a core set of activities surviving today, including Local History, Photovision, Bookgroup, Languages, and more. The Covid pandemic disrupted meetings, and particularly physical activities (Badminton, Ballroom Dancing), though some still operated via Zoom. Against all odds, u3a on Arran not only survived the pandemic, but actually thrived.

Today we have a flourishing Arran u3a, with our own ukulele and fiddle groups entertaining members at monthly meetings. New groups have been added, including Film Group, Outdoor Art and Tech Savvy.

The Writing Group has been meeting for over a year now, with members writing in response to monthly prompts from moderator Barb Taub and other members of the group. Last summer, the group was invited to attend workshop presentations at the Arran Writers' Retreat. This anthology showcases the endeavours of this vibrant group.

# Contents

# A V Dunne

## THE WIFE, THE MISTRESS, AND THE GUINEA PIG ° NEW BEGINNINGS ° A LIFE IN LISTS ° DANCING IN THE KITCHEN °

### About A V Dunne

Anne considers herself to be generically Scottish, having grown up in the Lothians and Ayrshire. She studied history at the University of Edinburgh. Many people assumed she was studying Literature, because she was either to be found in the English section of the library or having a nap on the deserted fifth floor where obscure books were stored. She was best known at university for being the girl who always had her dog with her. Anne's life has been filled with pets since childhood — hamsters, rats, guinea pigs, a rescue chicken, a crow, horses and pedigree sheep. She has never been without a dog or two. Anne has now settled on Arran with a labrador and a border collie. Both are tolerant of her scribbling. They find it far less traumatic than her singing phase.

# The Wife, The Mistress, and the Guinea Pig

There is no concept, nor definition of normal, when you are a child. Growing up in a family, your family is your normal. Perhaps, in later years, when you look back as a fully formed and questioning adult, you might realise that aspects of your childhood did not conform to the usual standards of the day. Then again, with families, as with marriages, outsiders cannot hope to fully comprehend the machinations and nuances of these units.

The family lived in a modest house, in a modest street and the children were oblivious to anything that set them apart. Mum, Dad, three girls, a boy, three dogs, a guinea pig and a hamster completed the family unit. The father, Alexander, was a small business owner. Elizabeth stayed at home with the children. The children might be somewhat scruffy, their clothes clean, but un-ironed. The house was generally messy, minimally hygienic but a comfortable family home. The children had been born in quick succession, each girl born a year and a day apart. September was an expensive birthday month in the MacDonald household. Kate, then Patricia and finally Alex, named after her father. Later, Mum would confess that having had three girls in three years the doctor had suggested that Mrs MacDonald might want to consider contraception. Having explained to her what it was, he wrote out the prescription and there followed three baby-free years before the family was completed by the arrival of the much yearned-for son, Paul.

The three dogs lived in harmony as an integral part of the MacDonald household. The eldest dog, Paddy, was a golden retriever who defied the recognised traits of his gentle breed and would attack strange dogs on sight. The next dog was a collie type of unknown heritage. A recognised Lothario, Toby could slip past any legs that tried to block a doorway or squeeze out any ground floor window. He'd fathered half the dogs in the neighbourhood and frequently stayed out all night, howling in some poor unfortunate's garden, serenading the love of his life imprisoned within. The third dog was a mistake. The children had been sent to buy a canary and came home with a puppy. Elizabeth had taken to her bed. Fanta lived to nurture. She regularly curled up amidst her litter of soft toys and brought them gifts of items stolen from the laundry basket. Guinea pigs were nuzzled and hamsters delicately groomed. The children were guarded, and their cuts and abrasions gently licked. Fanta was a frustrated mother and loved nothing more than snuggling up with the free-range guinea pig on the hearth.

Elizabeth might not have been the perfect housewife. The household was chaotic, the children semi-feral, the dogs out of control and Elizabeth herself attired in scruffy, mismatched clothes – fashion held no interest for her. However, Elizabeth had found her vocation. She mothered the children and the animals. She nurtured, supported and took pride in them all and loved her husband. She solved the family's problems.

Paddy was walked only after dark and had a collection of tree branches stored at the garden gate. Elizabeth understood that Paddy would be reluctant to drop his treasure if they should encounter a strange dog.

Toby had his identity disc removed in order to avoid possible paternity suits.

The children too had their quirks. Kate was slow to speak, therefore the family became fluent in Beep Beep Booby, her chosen language.

Patricia cursed like a trooper. Her mouth was washed out with soap to clean it up.

Alex loved to read, and it was accepted that she should be given the space to consume one or two children's novels a day.

Paul hated wearing pyjamas. In the hour or two before bedtime, he sat with the rest of his family enjoying television – bare naked.

Some problems Elizabeth couldn't solve on her own. The garden had become an overgrown wilderness. Even Paddy's collection of tree branches was becoming inaccessible. Alexander was not inclined to garden, nor was Elizabeth.

There wasn't enough money to pay a professional, and neighbours had been coming to the door to complain.

This time it was Alexander who came up with a solution. His friend, Lisa, was a keen gardener. She would come and sort out the verdant jungle, liberate Paddy's Pile and perhaps plant some flowers.

Lisa was not unknown to the children. She played a satellite role in family life. They'd holidayed at the same caravan park. When Elizabeth was hospitalised, the children and Alexander had decanted to Lisa's house. Once, she'd arrived at the house and there had been shouting and Elizabeth had cried. The children understood that their father was with them on Mondays, Tuesdays and Wednesdays, but spent Thursdays, Fridays and Saturdays at Lisa's house. It made their Mum unhappy at times, but as children, they had no concept that this was an unusual set up for family life. Dad came back on Sundays to take them swimming and let Mum have a few hours to herself. The normal family routine resumed.

Solution found. Lisa would come and sort out the garden the following weekend whilst Alexander was at work.

To give Lisa her due, she might have been a potential homewrecker, but she worked like a Trojan on that garden. She hacked and she sawed, she dug out weeds and she hauled away the debris of MacDonald life. In six hours or so, it had been beaten into submission. Admittedly, there were no borders planted with pretty flowers, but the fence was visible, and Paddy's collection of tree branches had been stacked beside the gate. Neither Elizabeth nor the children had offered to help.

Good manners ensured that Lisa was invited in for a cup of tea, but she lacked the good manners or insight to politely decline. She was seated on the worn sofa, looking disdainfully at the detritus of family life. A curtain had come off the rail, a glass of blackcurrant juice had been spilled on the arm of the sofa. The floor was littered with toys and felt pens. The three dogs had curled up on a rug beside the sleeping form of Paul. He was wearing pants. Two pairs.

One pair around his waist and the second pair on his head. Clean laundry had been folded and placed on chairs. The guinea pig, Leroy, settled on top of one such pile assessing the visitor.

Lisa was handed a cup of tea. No chipped mug for this visitor, but rather the last remaining cup and saucer from the MacDonald's wedding china. Elizabeth was notorious for dropping crockery and it was rare for her to wash up without breaking something. Awkward conversation followed.

Leroy was quite a dominant, but loving guinea pig. The children hugged and played with him endlessly, but the dogs knew better than to try and take his beloved carrot from him. Fanta would gaze at him as he munched, but never approached until he'd eaten his fill. When he walked away and abandoned the last of the carrot, Fanta would nip in, grab it and munch the tasty morsel.

Leroy completed his assessment of the visitor. He moved from his nest on top of the laundry, and from the arm of the chair to the sofa. He approached Lisa. She made all the right noises about how adorable and friendly he was. She gently stroked his handsome head as he sat on her lap. Leroy was not fooled. He paused in his ascent to her shoulder and sank his rodent teeth deeply into her left breast.

Lisa screamed in shock and pain to the amusement of the family. The best china cup flew through the air. The scalding tea cascaded over Lisa: heaping agony upon agony. Elizabeth bundled Leroy into her arms, apologised profusely and scolded the recalcitrant rodent. She removed him to the kitchen. Alex followed a few minutes later. Leroy was on Elizabeth's lap being smothered in kisses and cuddles and fed the tastiest of titbits.

Lisa left without accepting the offer of a replacement cup of tea.

A decade later, when the older children were at university, Alexander and Elizabeth's marriage failed and he moved into Lisa's house permanently. He still came once a week to visit, and never left without kissing his wife goodbye. They held hands as they attended graduation ceremonies. At some point Alexander told Patricia that the time had come for him to marry Lisa. A divorce was pending. He explained that he and Lisa had been together for twenty-five years. Patricia pointed out that for half of that time he had been married to and living with her mother. After the divorce he continued to visit the family home and kiss Elizabeth goodbye.

Alexander was the first to die. Elizabeth and Lisa sat together in the first funeral car and the children followed in the second. Both wives maintained sporadic contact and exchanged birthday cards and Christmas gifts.

The family ensured that transport was arranged in order to allow Lisa to attend Elizabeth's funeral. Thereafter, the children kept in touch and visited occasionally. After all, family was important, and they were the only family Lisa had.

The MacDonald family definition of normal was perhaps unusual, but the children were not traumatised. They grew up loved, nurtured and protected from adult tensions and stresses. They were taught forgiveness and compassion.

They learned never to underestimate the emotional intelligence of guinea pigs.

# New Beginnings

Tall walls.
Tall windows.
Tall ceiling.
Small me.

Thirty round faces.
All strangers.
The teacher.
A lady.
Unknown to me.

Five years at home.
No playgroup.
No nursery
No nights at Grandma's.

Just Mummy.
And Daddy.
My brother and sisters.
Everyone I needed and loved under one roof.

Low walls.
Low windows.
Low ceiling.
Safe me.

Plucked.
Scared.
Alone.
Abandoned.

What to do?
Choices?
Cry?
Wet my pants?

I did both.

# A Life in Lists

"Is it time for bed?" asked Mum for the eighth time.

"No, Mum." she replied. "We've just had lunch. You can go for a wee nap if you like. I need to go to the shops anyway."

"Are you sure? I saw some bats flying outside."

"I think you must have seen some birds, Mum. You don't usually see bats this early in the day."

She looked out the window. Even the weak winter sunshine was enough to reveal how dusty the glass was. Another job to add to her list.

Craig wandered into the kitchen clutching his new puppy. The pup had arrived ten days ago, and its feet had barely touched the ground. Craig tended to hold it to his chest most of the time. Not ideal, and it was playing havoc with her efforts at house training. She'd have to sort that out, but for the moment the awkward man-child moved from room to room with his tiny puppy held closely to him at all times. They both looked a bit lost and confused.

"I'm off to the shops." she said. "Do you need anything?" she asked.

He grunted something in reply. It seemed to indicate a negative response to her query. Why did adolescents lose the ability to communicate and choose not to pronounce any consonants?

She sat at the kitchen table taking refuge in writing her list. Keeping everything organised. Staying in control and ensuring that the family continued to function.

- Food shopping

- Pick up Mum's prescriptions

- Order feed for the horses

- Arrange puppy vaccination

- Phone work

- Cancel Mum's chiropody appointment

- Clean the bloody window – Maybe that would scare the bats away and Mum would stop pestering her to help get her into her pyjamas.

"Will you keep an eye on Nana?" she asked. Another grunt. This one seemed to indicate an affirmative response and boy and puppy exited the kitchen.

"I'm off then. I won't be long, Mum. Craig's at home and you can go for a nap. Remember, you've got your red button to press if you fall or need help."

Too late she realised her mistake. Mum immediately looked down to the pendant hanging around her neck, as if noticing it for the first time, and pressed the red button. The phone automatically dialled the monitoring service to alert the falls team.

Twenty minutes later she'd made it into the car. The falls team had been appeased, Mum was safely tucked in for a nap, Craig and puppy were slouched on a chair playing something inappropriately violent on the games console. She decided to go to a different supermarket. She really didn't want to bump into anybody she knew.

She'd half-filled the trolley. It was taking forever walking up and down unfamiliar aisles picking up all the usual items. Referring to her list.

Her list was her downfall. Her source of comfort ultimately caused her to come undone. Her list broke her.

Coffee, it said. She didn't need coffee. Mum drank tea. She and Craig only drank juice. She might never need to buy coffee ever again. The tears came quietly and flowed freely. She'd learned just to let them come – to let them be. It was less messy than rubbing at already swollen eyes with rough tissues.

She walked away from the trolley and didn't feel any

remorse at abandoning the frozen food to its fate. She drove the short journey home. Still not tempted to wipe the tears away. Home safely.

"What's wrong? What's happened?" Craig asked. She explained about the coffee. He understood. He got it. He assured her he'd accompany her to the shops the next time.

Mum wandered in. It upset her to see her daughter cry. Soon she was settled with her mug of tea in her special white, china mug. The radio played quietly in the background.

"Where's Allan?" Mum asked.

She spoke gently. "Allan died Mum. Remember?"

"Oh no. How could I have forgotten. I'm so sorry. I'm so sorry. Do you want me to go home? I'll manage on my own. You can't look after me as well as everything else."

"Please, Mum. Stay here. Don't leave. I need you more than ever. I need you here." she pleaded. Mother and daughter held hands across the table. Taking comfort in each other's touch.

Craig got up to move. He struggled to deal with this raw emotion. He had his pup to help him through. He'd named him Hetzer. He and his dad had played some online tank games and had agreed that it would be cool to call the puppy after a German tank. Hetzer had arrived last Friday. Allan lay on the couch waiting. Excited at the prospect of the new arrival, but tired. Very tired. He met Craig's puppy and fell asleep with the Hetzer cradled in his arms.

On Saturday Allan stayed in bed. Over the next few days, the house was quiet. Family, friends, doctors and nurses came and went. The minister visited. When the undertakers arrived, Craig insisted on accompanying them to the hearse - all the time holding on to his puppy. Their puppy.

Mum was settled. Craig was back online. She'd have to prepare a meal soon that nobody would eat. She'd add food shopping to tomorrow's list and Craig would come with her. She still needed those lists.

Tomorrow's list:

- Email eulogy to minister
- Return unused morphine to pharmacy
- Take clothes to undertakers
- Phone Craig's school with funeral details
- Decide on pall bearers
- Visit Allan's Mum
- And food shopping

# Dancing in the Kitchen

I miss someone who understands how to restart
the wifi.
I miss someone who stacks the dishwasher like a
professional.
I miss someone who worries I'll check their
spelling when they scribble a holiday postcard.
I miss someone who undertakes cleaning the
bathroom as if it were a military operation.

I remember trips on a motorbike and pretending
I enjoyed them.
I remember that first flat and how cold it was.
I remember a white dress, flowers and wedding
vows.
Till death us do part.
And it did.

I miss resting my head on your shoulder.
I miss ending every day with "Night, night. I love
you."
I miss you kissing the tip of my nose.
I miss dancing in the kitchen.

# Anne Hodge

## SPINDRIFT ° EMMA'S GIFT ° GIRL TALK ° LOSS ° CONIC HILL ° KAIROS

**About Anne Hodge:**

I am a twin. We are 85 years old. I have lived for most of my life near the sea. I am passionate about dooking[1] daily throughout the year. I enjoy the company of dogs and Archie, a tiny terrier visits me. I go daily to be with a tortoise and when she sees me she dashes over to receive the dandelion leaves and flowers that I bring. She's about my age.

---

1. Dooking, in Scotland, means to dip or plunge into the sea. It is NOT for the fainthearted.

## Part One: Spindrift, Whiting Bay

1st April 2012

Dear Eileen,

Till yesterday I was worried because I thought I loved sailing in my new man's boat, the Spindrift, more than him. But it's all the other way round now. Early yesterday we sailed south from Gigha in order to be with the tide at the Mull of Kintyre.

It was a lovely morning, and a light breeze aided us. Dolphins leapt, crisscrossing ahead of the bow. They made sweet wooshing noises. I made coffee and knitted in the cockpit. Feeling tired, I left Ian steering to go below for a nap. Ian was on watch, doing a crossword and splicing ropes.

I woke up feeling cold, hearing waves crashing on the bow. I popped my head out and I couldn't see Ian. "Where are you?"

"Here, taking in the sails. It'd s bit rough, come out and steer for a minute?"

Pulling on my life jacket I joined him in the cockpit. It was cold, misty and windy. The seas were lumpy. The wind was strengthening from north and west. In no time we were in a gale. When we crashed round the Mull, the seas were overwhelming, but then the wind changed to north. We were very cold.

Eileen, I'm afraid I started to cry, I was so scared. These huge waves and a horrid mist were not normal.

A fishing boat loomed up behind us and stayed close for a bit. They wanted to talk to us on the radio but I was too scared to go down. We were now motoring. I sat on the floor of the cockpit and puked into Ian's sowester. I didn't want the fishermen to see me but I banged my mouth on the steering equipment and bled.

Ian said "It's a shame."

At one point a yacht came towards us sailing comfortably, yet it was bashing into the waves which had gone back to southwest.

Once we were finally round the Mull well and truly, we were hungry and drank cognac and ate ginger biscuits! We out up a little bit of the jib. Ian steered with my head on his knee and sang "Bear me over the seas to Arran". He had a lovely soft tenor voice and we sailed up to Campbelltown to the pontoons.

We had a wonderful afternoon tea in the Royal Hotel. You must come sailing soon.

Yours ever,

Sister Anne

## Part Two: Muck!

Anne's letter asking her sister to join them for a sail among Scottish islands makes its way south. Finally it reaches a hill in North Norfolk, where a street boomerangs downwards The street is bordered on either side by neat houses; only a handful of them are old and their walls are pebble studded. Gardens are generous and well cared for, yet the occupants are elderly; some houses are holiday homes. Evenings are quiet; television screens flicker.

In a house at the top, Eileen and Kevin are packing for a special holiday.

"Eil, I'm whacked - ready to give in. Take all your paraphernalia off the bed."

"Oh, Kevin - have you packed properly? What about towels,

waterproofs and wellies?"

"I have no wellies, I'm taking my trek sandals."

"Well, I think you should have a final check; we're leaving at dawn."

"Yes, hardly worth going to bed." Kevin pushes himself underneath the cluttered duvet, and is snoring in no time at all.

Eileen eventually completes her packing and drags two great grips – gaping widely – down the hall. The plan is to join Eileen's sixty-six year old twin sister in Ardrishaig, which is at the start of the Crinan Canal, on the west coast of Scotland. Anne has a partner who owns a yacht.

"She's called "*Femme Fatale,*" Anne informed them, although lots of Scots read the name aloud, pronouncing it - *femmy fatilay*.

Eileen and Kevin have little previous sailing experience. So their job, sister Anne informed them, will be to work the locks on the canal. There are fifteen locks and for two of them there is no work to be done because a lock keeper assists.

Late afternoon on day one, Anne and Ian have sailed all the way to Ardrishaig from Lamlash, on the Isle of Arran. Anne is worried when she doesn't see her sister. "Oh dear, there's no sign of them but the lock keeper will see us up the first lock and we can stay in the basin for the first night. Are you looking forward to seeing them, Ian?"

"No, you know I don't like a crowd aboard and Eileen will have lots of bags. You have heaps of extra stuff as it is, including a fiddle, books, and knitting. And there are all the things to come that you'll pick up in Charity and Craft shops."

"Don't worry, the car will be close by, we'll put things in the boot."

No sooner have they tidied up in the basin, than Eileen and

Kevin appear.

Eileen shows Anne a dark blue hyacinth vase. "We've been to the Charity Shops in Lochgilphead."

Anne feels a spasm of envy.

Later they enjoy a pub supper. As they stroll back to the boat Kevin asks intelligent questions about his duties on the next day.

Ian, the captain, has the entire rear cabin; where he sits, sipping a glass of red wine. The main cabin has no space for him. Eileen and Kevin are lying in their sleeping bags on either side of the table.

Anne is heating their hot milky drinks in the galley. She says, "It will work splendidly if we all help one another and are kind and considerate."

Kevin doesn't hear, he's asleep before his drink is ready. And when Anne lies down in the fore cabin, fitting herself around her goods, she marvels at how rhythmical the snoring of Eileen and Kevin is. "Kevin, Eileen, Kevin, Eileen; I can't even hear Ian."

Visiting the heads in the night is difficult. Everyone goes twice and the floor is strewn with spectacles, torches, teeth, pills and eye drops. A cool windy morn awaits the crew. There's time for a quick buying spree in a second-hand shop next to the canal, and then the twins are ready to do their bit.

Kev, who wakens at five every day, has attempted to go ashore for a shower; alas, he takes too long a step from ship to shore and the boat rail knives into him. He is consequently in pain. Between each lock, he walks to his car and drives it up to the next lock. By the time he has driven the car well up the canal side, left it and walked back, he's still in pain and longs to be seated or home with his lap top. Kevin is sixty-nine; and while he has always lacked coordination, he's eager to sail.

"Oh dear, Ian, look at him. Eileen, tell him to push with his back."

Eileen goes to help Kevin and shouts back, "We'll work together, Kevin's way. He's a bit scared that he may fall into the canal."

A gin palace, an enormous white motor boat with its partying passengers, is their companion boat in each lock. She sways all over the place and sends out a choking set of fumes from her twin engines, which are just ahead of *Femme Fatale*. Anne tries to fend off the big brute as it threatens to bump the *Femme Fatale*. "If only Eileen was helping here, I've so much to do. Can we stop in the middle, Ian?"

"No, let's keep going. They've only one week, I hope," he mutters.

By the late afternoon, they've passed through about fifteen locks. Kevin, who has walked the nine miles moving the car from lock to lock, and helped with each lock, looks exhausted.

"Now Kevin, take the sheet from the bollard and drop it to me."

Kevin gazes down, puzzled.

"Now, Kevin, the rope," she repeats. "From the dock."

"What do you want, Annie?"

"You'd think that by now he'd know what to do," says Ian loudly.

Kevin lifts the rope loops from the hook and he appears to be trying to tow the yacht forward; interested onlookers watch.

"Kevin, PASS DOWN THE F------ ROPE NOW!"

Kevin drops it into the water ahead of the prow. As Anne pulls it out, she hears an onlooker say to Kevin, "Aw, that's a shame, son. You wis just tryin' to be helpful."

Eileen is cross too. Her man is tired and he's in pain. He drove a lot of yesterday and today he's walked and opened and shut sluices. Doesn't Anne realise he's a bit hard of hearing? Eileen too is feeling whacked. In the night she was alarmed because the boat was so still. Was it still afloat? What if the water had drained away?

Anne is watching their unenthusiastic crewmates. "Oh dear, Ian, they both look unhappy and tired."

At the last lock Eileen comes aboard. Holiday makers are there in huge numbers on the gin palace ahead of them. Anne takes a vow, "I won't swear."

The sea is just beyond the last hurdle. Kevin is driving to Ardfern, the last stop. Just as the boat is ready to motor forth, Anne, who is standing in the prow sorting ropes, calls to Eileen in the familiar bossy way only a sister can claim, "Fend port side, now to stern – quick to starboard."

"Fend it yourself." Eileen sits down.

Ian is so taken aback by Eileen's reply that he loses steerage. Starboard side crashes into the whinstone walls and the boat grinds her way out to the sea at Crinan.

As *Femme Fatale* sails north, the twins make up. They see an otter swimming close to the shore and suddenly it flicks its elastic body up and dives.

"It's the way you speak to us, Anne."

"I know, I'm sorry; it's just the stress of it all."

They all try hard to have fun on their travels, but it is difficult.

Ian is grumbling to Anne.

"Why doesn't Kevin move out of the way when we're putting up our sails?"

"Do they need to bring all that junk aboard night after night?"

"Why do they start talking at five o'clock in the morning?"

"Well, Ian," Eileen asks her own questions. "Why don't you consult us before you decide where and when to eat? There are four of us here."

"Kevin, you seem to sleep with no worries to wake you." says Eileen. "Last night, on anchor here in Tobermory, I felt as if the anchor had dragged. I woke up Annie, she didn't even get up to look. She said, 'Och you have these night fears. Look out the port hole and you'll see we aren't budging.' But I couldn't see as the glass is so weathered."

Next day they are all ashore. The men down a pint or two in the Mishnish and Eileen yields to temptation and buys a necklace of freshwater pearls with a green semi-precious heart-shaped stone dangling from the centre. Eileen and Anne take advantage of being the first aboard to have a secret gloat over the lovely jewels down in the cabin. There is little time as the men are approaching in the wee red dinghy. They hear its motor stop. The twins stuff the necklet (bought with Kevin's savings) into a spare toilet roll and giggle.

There's a shout from Ian followed by desperate calling, "Eil, Eil, quick, help me."

Michty, Kevin is partly submerged. He clings with both hands to a handle on the stern. Eileen rushes to the stern, her voice as panicked as Kevin's. "Oh dear, he'll get Weil's Disease if he goes right in, he'll be swimming through the motions."

The twins grab a shoulder each and exhort Kevin to raise a leg to the platform. It's soon obvious, he can't raise anything. He clings to the stern, a distressed, bespectacled Neptune with a wet beard and expression of anxious sadness. Ian is powerless but if Anne lets go for a jiffy, she can place a rope around him.

"Don't let go, Annie," Kevin beseeches her.

But lo! A capable man from the boat *Alert* approaches in his big soft dinghy. "Roll over to me, sir – you must let go NOW." And with a swirl of dirty sea water, Kevin is aboard this dinghy.

After this Eileen and Kevin want to make for Oban in the bus and ferry and meet up with their Astra. Ian wants them to do it.

"One more sail," begs Annie, "we've never been to Muck; it's near and sounds lovely."

Everyone feels good sailing by Ardnamurchan Point and onto Muck. The wind is from the west, force four or five, Ian thinks. Then Eileen's a shade queasy.

"Take the helm, Eil; you'll feel better," Anne urges, and Eileen does. They sail right to the buoys marking the way in for the ferry. In the harbour there is no wind and plenty of sunshine.

After a quick cup of tea they row ashore and are delighted to find a restaurant. "Can we book an evening meal, please?"

"Yes, but come at eight; we've six bookings already."

Ian returns to the boat for a sleep and the others take the tar road over the island and they see Rum and Eigg. Down they go on to the north side of the little island and enjoy a swim in the second bay they come to.

"Isn't it clean, Kevin?"

"Isn't it all glorious," he replies.

They meet a handful of friendly, relaxed folks. One bike passes. The houses fit the landscape. Kevin is thrilled when he sees puffins on the cliffs; then he spots razor bills, shags, and a raft of eiders who coo and murmur in the warm sea.

"If only we could name the wild flowers, there are so many," says Eileen.

Anne thinks she could name all of them, but decides not to be a know-all.

Later their meal is delightful; fresh fish in a lemon sauce, new potatoes and wild raspberries.

As the men listen to the other yachtie folks' tales of the sea, the twins wander into the Craft Shop by the kitchen. They buy a painting and a book of poems by Meg Dewar, who long ago, before they were born, enjoyed the loveliness of Muck.

And as the four nestled down in their bunks, they feel

thoroughly blessed.

Muck has set the crew of the *Femme Fatale* to rights.

# Emma's Gift

On a box of sticks,
In a corner of the porch, lay six white tulips.
Taking them one by one from their wrapping of green leaves
I pierced each delicate neck through
With a fine gold pin.

Tired of the task
I pushed the bunch down
Into a blue bulb vase.

Sad looking, an instant change was needed.

Now they paddle
In grass green glass.

## Girl Talk

"**O**h let's not be ratty. We're bound to disagree. We can't talk about it and air our views without disagreeing. Let me order - what would you like?"

Edna, who had been slouching in her seat, was interested in the cafe. "Well it's your turn - a black coffee please." Smiling, she added, "It will waken me up for the night ahead."

The cafe on the top floor of Macys was enormous, so big that the folk at the other end looked small.

Janice caught the eye of the nearest waitress. She clumped across the hard floor and took their order. "Earl Grey for one and a black coffee, please."

Edna grimaced. "I shudder when you order Earl Grey. You do know that it smells of lavatory cleaner?"

"Does a bit." Janice laughed. "Funny thing is I used to loathe it, but one day I drank it by mistake and really enjoyed it. Does your palate alter like that? Take sweets. I ate so many as a kid that I lost all my teeth. Never touch them now."

"Oh, for heavens sake, talk about the bloody film."

"Well OK, here are the drinks." Janice waved away the waitress. "No, keep the change." Stirring sugar into her tea, she returned to Edna's question. "Tell me, why did you hate the film?"

"I didn't just hate it. I can't see how anyone could have enjoyed it. The drab scenes, the contrived grimaces – I could just imagine the Director telling her to practice the pathetic walk. So ungainly. What prostitute ever walked like that?"

"Well I can't understand you Edna, I was enthralled from the time she was pushed into the river to the time when she marched down the road with strangers and that brave smile was on her face. It was a film about the power of the human spirit. Such a pretty girl too."

Sipping her black coffee, Edna grudgingly said, "The clothes were inappropriate for the fifties. And her bedroom! - it was like a film star living in a hut, though it was all she had apart from her radio and budgie."

Janice pretended to look worried. "Will it make us afraid of the punters tonight? Should we take a night off?"

Edna smiled suddenly "What, go home to lie beside my drunken husband in that creaky old bed? No, I'd rather walk into the river."

The friends stood up and linked arms as they approached the cash desk. After, they turned to the glass bubble, a lift that skimmed down the outside of the building. They entered together, still talking, but as the elevator plunged down, both friends reached for the railing and braced their feet. At the ground floor, Edna and Janice walked out into the night air.

"I really feel ready to do a good job tonight." Janice stepped out ahead of Edna. The two friends headed to their work at Fellini's pole dancing.

# LOSS

Four men
A father
Three sons
Stand
Shoulder grasping
A ring
Of grief

# Conic Hill

We've saved up all our energy, we're going to climb that hill.
It's not a mountainous huge one, but topping it will thrill.
Park the car, lace up the boots, take bags and sticks and sweets
Visit the three-door building, then tramp on willing feet.
We're running through the woods; the air is very still
Leaves land on us from above, yet pines grow on this hill.
Reaching a gate - NO DOGS we read. Our Susie's having fun.
"It isn't lambing time," says Dad. "No threat from shepherd's gun."
"I'll take her back," says Grampa. "We'll both sit in the car.
And I shall read the Herald and think, "How lucky we two are."
The path goes ahead and upwards. Granny is quite flushed.
"Lets pause and see the view, I feel so very puffed."
This hummock must be the last climb, no need for weans to halt.
"We're on conglomerate," gasps Gran. "The Highland Boundary Fault."
At last we rest on the summit, picnicking and gazing afar.
"See the tower blocks of Glasgow."
"Race you down to Balmaha."

# Kairos

*"I was much too far out all my life, and not waving but drowning."*
– STEVIE SMITH, FROM COLLECTED POEMS OF STEVIE SMITH 1972

*Water water wall flower*

*Growing up so tall.*

*We are all children*

*And we must all die.*

*Except Jeanie Deans*

*The youngest of us all.*

*She can dance and she can sing.*

"And she can... and she can... What?" Jeanie wondered. "What was the last bit?"

Never mind, she'd think of another playground rhyme. "One potato, two potatoes, three potatoes, four..." She said it all.

It was great how she could still see the faces of the girls who'd been in her school ninety years ago, see them bobbing up and down in the ropes and when they'd to stop skipping, how cleverly they'd run out as another girl darted in.

Poor Peggy, standing cawing the rope for the entire playtime. The other end was tied to a hook on the wall. Peggy had never been well. She wasn't allowed to try skipping because she had rheumatic fever when she was six, and she couldn't cope with school work. She just liked cawing.

On a hot summer day when Peggy was ten years old, she went to the beach at the pier to paddle while the other children, clad in moth-eaten woollen costumes, bathed. Jeanie remembered the laughter when two bathers came wearing combinations. They were chased into deeper waters. She could hear the shrieks and screams and laughter yet. But suddenly the children were ordered out of the water by the pier master. He sent them all home and later they learned that Peggy had gone out of her depth and drowned. Jeanie's dad said, "Puir wee lassie, she was too far out and not waving." And that was long before Stevie Smith wrote her poem.

Now Jeanie was having to leave the home and the island and be taken to another Old Folks' Home far away on the mainland. All her life she had lived on Arran. She'd outlived all the girls in her class, and she expected that the boys were dead and gone. "I could try to jump off the ferry, but some idiot would stop me, or jump in after me."

Funny how her thoughts today were all jumbled and hearkening back to the far-off past; but she knew that today was the day to face the big change, the new place. "Where shall I go for a wee walk? I've walked by the sea all my days. I'm a bit tottery now but I must be by the sea. Oh, but I'm proud that I've outlived so many and lived for a hundred years on Arran. And I thank God for my life, when I'm homesick for Arran, I'll just remember."

But sitting on the ferry, tears crept down her face. An old man sitting at her side was smoking a filthy pipe. They were seated in the recliner NO SMOKING lounge and he said, "Are you Jeanie Deans? We were in the same class. Peter Campbell."

Peter Campbell! And in an instant she remembered Peter; saw him standing facing the class. And she saw and heard Miss Hume say, "Watch the class Peter and if any children talk or stop writing, put their names on the blackboard. I'll be back when I've reported Alex's diarrhoea to Mr. Birch."

Jeanie remembered that the teacher was away for ages and poor Peter had been so upset at the unruly behaviour of the class that he had wet the floor, then the class were quiet and stared at Peter whose face turned bright red. Jeanie had felt sorry for him.

Now he said, "Where do you think we'll fetch up today?"

"I don't know, Peter. Maybe we'll have a pleasant surprise. Let's think of it as a holiday and we can talk a lot about our lives on Arran."

They could not see their island home from their low seats but they thought of it, left behind, and Jeanie said to herself, "Dying will be easier than this."

*Kairos – Greek word for a unique time in a person's life, an opportunity for change.*

# Helen McIntosh

## CHEESE PRESSING ° BRUSHES WITH DEATH

### About Helen McIntosh

Helen McIntosh is a former University Lecturer — mother of two, grandmother to four — who lives happily in Whiting Bay on the Isle of Arran. After retiring on medical grounds, she became an active member of the University of the Third Age on Arran as a committee member (Group Co-ordinator) and as a group leader to two groups.

# Cheese Pressing

Accompanying the Business Studies students on their week's Outward Bounding course seemed like a sensible idea. I could get to know some of them better and could help them in my role as placements tutor. We endeavoured to get them working as teams — planning activities, leading, lateral thinking, and more — so the activities themselves were designed to get participants out of their comfort zones.

I was well out of my own comfort zone just by being there, sharing a dormitory, sleeping on the top bunk bed, and not being sure what exactly my role was. I soon found an additional zone of discomfort on the first evening, as I got to know the ten students in my group, which included three boys from Northern Ireland. I knew we would have to go out on a bivouac night which involves the students building their shelter from a couple of tarpaulins and some ropes. I didn't count on it being the first night at Ullswater.

Before setting off, we were briefed by our group leader, a gentle giant who took us across the lake in a small boat in the dark. In the pitch black night, we saw little of our surroundings, merely listening to the rhythm of the outboard motor, alongside the chatter of the students. This being the end of October, it was cold and we only had three functioning torches between us, though thankfully sleeping bags were provided. One unfortunate boy slipped in the water as we landed (just his feet got wet), but we all soon got used to being wet and cold on that memorable week. The Centre was warm and comfortable, and — surprisingly for mass catering — the food was good. Thankfully, the showers were soothing and warming to bodies subjected to several hours in the cold and wet, along with more and more bruises on our limbs as the week progressed.

My night-camping team of students was split into two groups, and left to locate a suitable 'tent' site — with their selected site, unfortunately, located in a gulley that gradually filled with water when the inevitable rain arrived. Having grown up with news stories about 'The Troubles' in Ireland, I can't describe the feeling, hearing what sounded like a small unit of the IRA, with the three Irish accents and the fact that all of them were wearing black balaclavas. Pete, the instructor, asked if I wanted to get into one of the student 'tents' or share his small tarpaulin that he slung between two trees, sloping down at an angle to allow one of us (me) to snuggle into. I opted to share, but questioned this when he said I'd benefit more from the sleeping bag if I took my clothes off. When his makeshift 'bivvy' blew down in the wind at 1:30am, I was glad to be still in my clothes.

Later in the week, having survived a night under the stars, listening to the laughs and screams of the students, we were taken caving to Alum Pot. For the trip, we were kitted out with wellies, helmets with functioning lights (this time), plus furry suits and oversuits to keep us warm. The claustrophobia didn't affect me, nor wading through water most of the way. But a waterlogged furry suit weighs a ton, and not being a size-10 myself, I found it hard to keep up with the youngsters. Pete had a 44-inch chest, so when we got to the infamous 'cheese press' passage, which he couldn't physically get through, he took me aside and asked delicately the size of my chest. I laughed and said my chest size wouldn't be a problem. But when I got stuck in the press, I shouted back that he should have asked about the size of my bum.

Near the end of this caving expedition, we encountered a large cavern with a sizeable pool in it. At one end was a waterfall, and to get out we had to climb up the waterfall aided by a rope. Exhausted, I sat at the edge of the pool and watched the students attempt to climb up the waterfall. Some made it easily, others had several attempts, falling back into the pool. At forty-odd years old, overweight, and bone-tired after having had very little sleep on the first night, followed by a day's activity including the demanding ropes course (don't ask), I thought I would never get out of there alive. So when it was my turn to climb, I gave a determined effort and — aided by one of the lovely Irish lads —got out at the first attempt.

As I sit here now in my seventies, I wonder what became of those three Irish boys who terrified me on my first night in camp, but turned out to be wonderful fellow campers.

## Brushes With Death

My first brush with death started on a drive up a twisty steep road in Tasmania, en route from Hobart – to Queenstown. I had the strangest sensation and started to feel ill. It had been a long time since I'd been travel sick, but after a brief stop at the summit of the road – a bleak lunar landscape – we descended down the road to stop at the Wilderness Railway (with me driving this time to combat the travel sickness).

I felt better after the break and with a wee bite to eat. I then drove the rest of the way to Cradle Mountain, where my companion (an old friend of the family) and I were going to see the New Year in. It was a strange resort made up of cabins, with one big communal area for dining etc. We were told under no circumstances to leave doors or windows open.

The resort blamed it on possums, but I suspect the snakes in the area were of greater concern. Before joining the Hogmanay party, we walked along a long boardwalk area through woodland, me stepping over a small snake. A man coming to meet us shivered and said, "I hate those things." I never found out if my little snake was a juvenile tiger snake or something benign. I also stopped on the boardwalk to say hello to a pademelon only a few feet away. We communed by eyeballing each other for what seemed like five minutes — a magical moment. The little marsupial wasn't scared and I was enchanted.

*PADEMELON: drawing by Amanda Lovejoy*

Although it was the Australian summer, Cradle Mountain boasted about having about 260 days of rain per year, and the weather was definitely not warm. I went out on New Year's day for an organised kayaking trip on Dove Lake, where our guide briefed us on one particularly venomous snake that roamed the area. He told the story of a young girl who had stopped for a toilet break, was bitten by this tiger snake on the bum, told no-one, and subsequently died. *Cheery story for the first of January,* I thought.

After a few days we travelled up to Launceston, from whence we took a flight back to Melbourne. It was probably the 4th or 5th of January that I started to get a headache. After three days with no respite, my friend John took me to a GP in the town of Camperdown, close to where he lived. I was given some pills which I subsequently threw up and went to bed. The next morning, John took me back to the doctor, who immediately wheel-chaired me to a local hospital. I haven't got a single memory of what followed until I woke up in St. Vincent's Hospital in Melbourne. Apparently, I had been transferred to another hospital in Warnambool, before the decision was taken to transfer me again to a specialist unit about three hours drive away.

My whole trip had been based around my visit to my daughter Sarah in Japan, with Australia and New Zealand as add-ons. I was due to fly back to the UK via Japan to visit Sarah once more. Strangely, she flew out from Tokyo to Australia on the very plane that would have taken me to her. She remained with me throughout the crisis period, when a female doctor apparently phoned my husband on Arran to tell him I was dying. They were initially puzzled by my deterioration as the bleed in the pineal region of my brain was minuscule, but enough to 'gum up' the channel through which fluid travelled. My life signs were definitely slipping off the radar when they rushed me into theatre. The surgical team drilled a hole in my skull to drain the viscous liquid that was shutting my whole system down. I immediately came back to life, apparently singing. The staff then supplied a selection of CDs including Nat King Cole's "Unforgettable", which now has a special place in my life with my lovely daughter.

I was by no means out of the woods during this period. To keep me alive, they had to keep the drain in my head open (apparently dangerous for infections). I was unable to see much of anything at this point, and came in and out of consciousness. I did, however, know that Sarah was with me. I hallucinated, telling Sarah this place had once been a hotel, and when I half-closed my eyes, I could see Rolf Harris in the curtains. (I don't believe there were curtains, and it was long before Harris was exposed as a sex fiend.) I also thought I was on some sort of outward-bound course with my daughter, with me lying on a low camp bed.

Someone must have talked about my husband coming out to Australia, and I got it into my head that he was arriving soon at the airport, and I needed to go and meet him. To expedite this, I pulled my catheter out, strangely not giving me any pain, but causing blood loss and lots of activity with the medical staff. As a result of my action they decided my hands would have to be tied down so I couldn't pull out the drain in my head. Again, strangely, this was the point at which I became agitated with my situation, and pleaded with my daughter to get them to remove the tethers. Actually, I remember now that I did manage to free my hands and asked Sarah not to tell them. She persuaded them to free my hands by promising to stay by my side to monitor my movements. They allowed her to sleep next to me for a period, but on one occasion persuaded her to get some proper sleep in another room. She insisted they tell her if I needed her. When I woke, alone and in the dark, I began to fret and shouted out for someone. Although Sarah couldn't have heard me from where she was, she miraculously came to me.

They sealed up the drain hole in my skull, and I was back in a fug again. They had to put the drain in one more time, before taking it out for good and leaving me with minor discombobulation. My daughter was going through my pictures and videos on my tiny Canon camera that I'd purchased in Japan at the beginning of my 'adventure'. She asked what these wee creatures were in so many of my stills and video shots. As I still couldn't focus, I said I didn't know, but they were of course Tasmanian devils - a species that is now under threat from a disease they infect themselves with through their aggressive fighting.

I remember a doctor asking my daughter if I smoked. She said no, but I interjected, saying I had that 'squiff' whilst in South Island, New Zealand (a story for another time). At some point during this period, my other daughter Gillian and my sister Sybil flew out to be with me and to help Sarah. My eighty-year-old dad also wanted to come, but they persuaded him to stay home. When my sister walked into my hospital room, I said, "You took your time". Considering how far she'd come, missing her 50th joint birthday party with my dad, to see her big sister and help out her nieces, I hope she now knows just what this meant to me.

I do remember the opportunity of a lifetime when the impossibly young brain surgeon asked if I had any questions.

"Will I be able to play the piano?"

"I don't see why not," Keith (Jones) replied.

"Good", said I gaily, "because I couldn't before."

I don't remember seeing much of my friend John, who had hosted me for about a month, showing me round Victoria and Tasmania, and who had got me to the doctor in the first instance. I found out later that he hated hospitals but was always around, looking after my girls and 'the auntie', finding them accommodation in the city. One of his friends, a politician in the Victorian parliament, lent his Melbourne flat for two weeks at one point. I do remember him coming to see me.

However, I owe a great deal to John, whose persistence in getting me medical help no doubt saved my life. Sarah reminded me of how, at the most critical moment of my decline, John and Sarah were summoned back to the hospital, and how he ran on arthritic limbs to be by my bedside.

Getting me back home was also a problem. At one stage, they talked about getting a jet to fly me to the UK. Fortunately, I'd taken out travel insurance for the three months I was away, and though the insurers tried to wriggle out of some of it, they paid for two nurses to fly out from England to bring me back on a first-class ticket. I don't remember the name of the nice one, but the other one was called Judy Garland. When we were introduced, I asked Judy if she'd seen him.

"Who?" she asked.

"The wizard, of course," I said. (Well, we were in Oz.) That may have been enough for her to dislike me, but considering my condition, it was no excuse for the pain she inflicted when taking out the oxygen feeds from my nose when I needed to go to the toilet on the flight home.

We stopped en route in Singapore, where there was a change of airline staff. My girls and the auntie were allowed off the plane but I had to stay put with my nurses. On the flight back to Heathrow, one of the hostesses took an interest in me, bringing the odd baby to see me (no doubt keeping both passengers amused on a long flight). The air steward was a lovely young woman from Glasgow and she was also on our flight from London. As we were just getting settled in our seats on this last leg of my journey (in fact the last time I was airborne), she approached me with a gift of orchids she'd bought in Singapore, saying they would brighten up my hospital bedside.  How lovely was that?

I was wheel-chaired towards the exit and met by my dad and a haggard, thin man I barely recognized as the husband I'd said goodbye to so many months before. He probably thought the same about me, and in fact my appearance probably caused my dad to faint whilst at the airport. The staff in Melbourne were pleased to know I would be going back to the world-renowned Glasgow hospital for neurology (they had developed the Glasgow scale for comas). Because my home address is on Arran however, they sent me to Crosshouse Hospital instead.

The contrast between the two hospitals couldn't be more stark. The wide-open spaces of St. Vincent's in Melbourne were now the cluttered spaces everywhere in the Ayrshire Hospital. But at least it was a welcome change from the tasteless food in the Australian hospital, which led me to ask my girls and my sister to bring in freshly squeezed juices, sushi and fresh fruit. On one occasion, 'the auntie' who was on duty with me made the mistake of arriving by my bedside with a fried egg roll. I salivated at this tasty morsel, and she had no option but to relinquish it to me. Seventeen years later she still refers to it, as she too was looking forward to a delicious piece of food, and thinks back wistfully to her lost bun.

Once ensconced in Crosshouse, I discovered another difference between my two hospitalisations. In Oz, whenever my hand was by my side, one of my three women held onto it. When I laid my hand on the bed with my husband by my side, the hand remained un-held, another example of the support I lacked during that dreadful time. He hadn't been taught to hand-hold. (On the plus side, the food in Crosshouse tasted of food — yum, yum.)

That was in January 2004. Fast forward to five or six years ago, when my husband decided he wanted to live on the mainland. As I did not, we agreed to a financial split of property, and off he went, first to the flat we had purchased in Glasgow, whilst owning the big house on Arran, and then to a nicer place in St Andrews. The deal was that we would split our time between here and there, still taking joint holidays. It took a while for me to notice that I was always the one to visit him. This worked for a while, but imperceptibly my health began to deteriorate. By May 2019, my next brush with death was beginning.

At first, I began falling over for no reason, and even listing to the side when sitting on a chair. I became incontinent, not willing to do much, and began to show signs of dementia. My GP prescribed pills for depression and incontinence. Most of the time I didn't seem to hurt myself when falling, but needed to be helped back up. Only once did I hurt my arm requiring a plaster for a small fracture, so I deduced I must have been collapsing like a drunken person most of the time. Fortunately, for me, I was relatively unfazed by this condition. But it must have been hell for my family, especially Sarah and her partner, who had to manage me, the children, running a large house, and more. Towards the end, Sarah had to put me into a residential home for respite care for short periods. People who encountered me at this time were baffled by my condition as I could be lucid some of the time, vacant at others and needed a barrage of social workers to help me to get up, back to bed, etc. At home, a bedroom was made up for me downstairs and various aids were put into the house to ease my passage from room to bathroom and back again.

During this period, Sarah watched a programme about dementia, hosted by Tony Robinson (Baldrick of Blackadder fame). It got her thinking and, more importantly, researching the internet. I remember vividly her coming into my room to tell me she thought she knew what was wrong with me. I was too far gone to be particularly interested in this information, but she pursued this diagnosis with medical professionals, eventually going private to a neurologist. This set the ball in motion, and I was finally taken into the Queen Elizabeth Hospital in May of last year for an operation to combat my 'normal pressure hydrocephalus'. *(NPH is an abnormal buildup of cerebrospinal fluid in the brain's ventricles.)*

The results were dramatic. Within a few days I was 'back to life'. A few weeks later, I was sent back to the Douglas Grant Rehabilitation Centre, where they couldn't believe the difference in me. There I met again with the psychologist who was so exasperated with me before my operation that she phoned Sarah on Arran to complain that I was not trying hard enough! Sarah then told her about her findings regarding my condition, to which she replied, "You are grasping at straws". Knowing about this interaction made it hard for me not to shout abuse at this woman. I merely told her that Sarah's diagnosis was correct, and flounced off. I'm pleased to say she no longer works at the centre as she was the only member of staff to unnerve me, all the others being caring and supportive.

My 'wet, wobbly and wacky' brush with death was over.

# William Henry

## It Takes The Cake ° The Road to Hell

### About William Henry

William Henry greatly enjoyed English Literature classes at school. His exposure to writing, other than personal letters to family and friends, was in writing the work based policy and procedure manuals connected with his employment. He enjoys relaxing with a good book (preferably on life in the Industrial Revolution) and suitable accompanying refreshment. He has never really grasped the internet.

# It Takes The Cake

"Well, that's the transfer completed. Let's drink to it."

Paul Richardson and his wife sat with a bottle of champagne before them on the garden table. They had arranged for their son to take over the management of their specialised engineering firm. Sylvia let her eyes wander over the flower beds. She had always had a sense of frustration in that the limited space restricted the colours and shapes of the plants she wanted to grow, Oh, to have some large old trees to provide homes for the birds, and maybe even a squirrel.

"You know Paul, I ask myself, wouldn't it be nice to live in the country? We don't have to be near our work any more."

Paul looked thoughtful. "It seems a good idea but I must admit I was thinking of a cruise to celebrate our retirement."

Sylvia smiled, "No. I have a better idea. Let's just drive around and see if we can find a country cottage. I keep seeing in my mind's eye that little village in the forest."

"In the forest?" Paul looked puzzled.

"Yes. Ribsdale. You know in the Forest of Bowland. It was a lovely old place. I remember the old stone cottages, some had dates going back to the 1600s carved over the doors. There was a lovely village green with that stream flowing through it and the ducks waddling down the middle of the road. It was a real old-fashioned place with proper shops - butcher, baker, greengrocer, post office, and the shop-keepers were so friendly."

"That's right," said Paul. "It had a fine old church and the clock chimed the hours. Real old-fashioned place. I remember we got a super meal at that pub opposite the village green."

The Richardsons duly set off on a tour of the Forest of Bowland, which lies between Preston and Lancaster. This was to be a journey of exploration. They would enjoy seeing the area, the geography, the plant and animal life, and buildings. And they wanted to know how the transport, healthcare and other services worked, and, last but not least, what was the social life of the area like?

Paul had started his working life as an apprentice in a Preston engineering firm which made machinery for the textile trade. He studied part time at the local technical college and eventually became a Member of the Institute of Mechanical Engineers. It was at the college that he met his wife Sylvia, who was studying Accounting and who became a taxation advisor in her own business. Both in their early sixties, the couple were active with many interests to occupy themselves.

Paul's hobby was building working models of steam locomotives and he was currently making a model of the Flying Scotsman. High on his list was space for his workshop and he had ambitions for a track running round a garden where he could have all his engines under steam.

Sylvia was noted for her green fingers and she had also produced many colourful embroidered pictures, based on her plants, which hung on their living room walls.

Both were keen gardeners, Paul worked the vegetable patch and his wife grew colourful flowers and cacti in her greenhouse.

On their first visit to Ribsdale, the Richardsons had been impressed with the food at the village pub and amused at its name. The Drake and Drummer was an unusual name for a pub, which was an old stone building, extended and altered in layout over several centuries. The garden had colourful flower beds interspersed with tables and benches.

The main bar welcomed regulars and visitors with its large open fire place and smoke-stained beams in its ceiling. Passageways led off to a large dining room used for events such as weddings and sporting club festivities. There were several smaller cosy rooms used by the bridge players, chess club, and small meetings.

The colourful pub sign across the front door featured a picture of a large white drake standing beside a drummer dressed in seventeenth century uniform of an infantry man beating his drum. A sign above the front door declared in gold print, *Edgar Howells, licencee, Good Beer, Good Food, Good Company.*

Paul and Sylvia explored the Forest of Bowland and agreed with the official classification as an Area of Outstanding Natural Beauty. More and more, they were attracted to Ribsdale as a retirement home.

"How is the search progressing?" their son, Peter, asked his parents. "My friend Ronald from the rugby team is an estate agent and is working with the builders of one of those new estates at Ribsdale. I'm sure he can give you a lot of information."

When they met, Ronald was able to tell Paul and Sylvia, " It's almost two villages now, old and new. The new has a school, two hotels as the area attracts many walkers, and public library and health centre. Old and new have a combined population of approximately 3,000 and they have grown together in the various clubs and societies which old and new alike join. There's a regular bus service to Preston and Lancaster, as most of those of working age commute. The housing is mixed local authority and private new build, and of course, the old village centre is full of ancient stone built dwellings."

This news spurred the Richardsons to begin a serious search for a new home in the old village and Ronald was asked to look for them.

Their next village visit was timed for lunch time so they could sample the food at the Drake and Drummer. A delicious smell of roast meat and the sounds of laughter and fiddle and guitar playing came from the bar. The landlord came over to their table.

"I'm Edgar Howells and you must be the people looking at Teasdale's cottage?"

Paul and Sylvia were amazed that it was known who they were. They were still only looking, not making a purchase at this stage. But now they knew the Drake and Drummer was the centre of knowledge on all things relating to life in Ribsdale. They soon discovered that nearly every club or association of villagers met for business in the pub and its patrons provided an ocean of knowledge as to what had happened, what was happening and what might happen in Ribsdale. It was difficult to keep a secret in the village.

The Richardsons moved into their new home soon afterwards and were quickly invited to join in village activities. New blood was always seized on to join the various committees and action groups.

The next big event in the village calender they soon learned, was the summer fete held in August, where many exhibitions of handicrafts and horticulture were held. The pet show was of particular appeal to the children.

The couple quickly settled into village life and learned that tradition played a large part in the events. Chairperson of the fete committee was the thrice widowed Mary Greenhalgh, a regular customer of the Drake and Drummer. A lady of substantial proportions, with her wiry grey hair and a strident voice, she appeared severe in her two piece tweed costume and strong outdoor shoes. Beneath this somewhat formidable appearance, however, she was generous in helping anyone in need, especially the mothers of young children.

As the time of the fete approached, Mary realised she had a problem. Two members of the committee suddenly decided to leave the village and go to live nearer their children in Devon.

"Hello, I'm Mary Greenhalgh and I want to welcome you to the village."

Sylvia stood in her open doorway and regarded the fierce-looking lady in front of her.

"It's very kind of you. We moved in last week and are still in a mess or I would invite you inside."

"Oh that's no problem, we have all the time in the world to do that sort of thing. Are you interested in gardening?"

"Well yes. Paul does the fruit and veg and I like to grow flowers. Why do you ask?"

"The village summer fete is on in a few weeks and there will be plenty of classes for both fruit and veg if you like to enter. Without entries, there would be no show."

Sylvia looked thoughtful. "I'm sorry but we really won't have time to produce anything this year. But if there is anything else we can do to assist, we will be delighted."

Mary had got the opening she wanted. "Well yes actually. Would you both come to a meeting this evening in the pub to finalise details? It's all very friendly and informal over a pint and a pie in front of the fire."

And so, even before their boxes were fully unpacked, the Richardsons were duly appointed to the village fete committee where, with Sylvia's experience in accounting, and Paul's in organising a business, their skills were immediately put to good use.

The great day approached and it was confirmed entries to the various classes would be five to seven pm the day before the fete, eight to ten am on the day of the show. Judging eleven am to twelve-noon on the great day.

Sylvia, who was now confirmed as Mary's deputy, did a final check of the baked goods to see the entries had been set out correctly. Sylvia and Mary awaited the arrival of the judge of the bread and cakes.

"It will be Mrs. Howarth," said Mary, "A lady of some renown - she is quite an expert on Victoria sponge cakes."

Sylvia was puzzled that, for once, Mary seemed in awe of another person. A sudden squawk and flapping of wings alerted them.

"What the hell," cried Mary, " It's a sodding pigeon."

Walking sedately amongst the sponge cakes was a plump pigeon. Grabbing a tea towel Mary rushed towards the bird which gave a loud squawk and took off, and hovering above a cake deposited its calling card on the cake.

"Bloody hell, it's shat on that cake!" wailed Mary. "What can we do? We'll have to cancel the cake contest. How can we explain this?"

Mary charged down the side of the table flapping the cloth and shouting, "Out. Out you bugger."

Sylvia took a deep breath. "Calm down, shut the door, and don't let anyone in. I'll be back soon. I'll give three knocks."

Sylvia set off at a fast pace whilst Mary sat shaking and muttering to herself. "What will we do? Do we scrap all these cakes, tell the Public Health, will we get fined? How do we tell people?"

*Knock, knock, knock.* Mary pulled the door open and Sylvia entered carefully carrying a basket.

"Put that cake in this plastic bag," commanded Sylvia. She surveyed the space where the soiled cake had stood. "No marks on the table. Good."

The soiled exhibit and the paper plate it had stood on now safely hidden in the plastic bag, Sylvia carefully took out a sponge cake and placed it on a new plate on the table. No sign remained of anything untoward having taken place.

"Say nothing," commanded Sylvia. "Just sit down and stop panting."

Some ten minutes later, a knock on the door indicated the arrival of Mrs. Howarth who diligently viewed, smelled, cut out a slice from each cake and placed award cards as appropriate. In front of cake brought in by Sylvia to replace the one soiled by the pigeon she placed a card proclaiming FIRST PRIZE.

"That's a good cake. Very good indeed."

Mrs. Howarth moved on and with a happy smile at Sylvia and Mary, set off to assess the home made wines. On her departure Sylvia took Mary's hand, and lead her out. After locking the hall door Sylvia said, "Right. A little something is what we both need."

A few minutes later seated outside the Drake and Drummer, a glass of whisky in hand the two ladies stared at each other.

Mary was the first to speak. "Marvellous, I can't believe it. You saved the day. Nobody will know what happened and your cake won first prize."

Sylvia laughed and shook her head. "No it's not my cake."

"Then whose is it?"

"Oh it's one I bought from Marks and Spencer. Bottoms up."

They drank deeply and laughed again.

To this day a stranger visiting the Drake and Drummer may find two ladies raise their glasses, toasting "To Marks and Spencer." And they would always break into laughter whenever "sponge cake" is mentioned in the pub.

Barbara Deacon, the lady who won the first prize for sponge cake at the village fete, could not resist bringing up the topic of "sponge cake" at the next gathering of the Rural Institute. She stood with her chest held out and bored the assembly in her high-pitched voice about how she made her prize-winning cake.

"She stands there with her chest puffed out just like a pigeon," said Lucy Bishop.

"And she squawks just like one," retorted Helen Green.

Mary and Sylvia burst out in laughter.

# The Road To Hell

Karen Morton and her husband Henry were with a group of friends in the Drake and Drummer. A log fire burned in the grate and a smell of roasting meat wafted into the lounge bar.

Amongst the chattering , Karen sat with a smile on her face staring at the fire.

"A penny for your thoughts," called out Debbie as she leaned forward and pushed Karen in the ribs. "Something on your mind?"

"Oh, what's that?" mumbled Karen.

"What are you thinking about? You don't seem to be with us," called Karen's brother Dick.

"It's the fire" responded Karen. "I like to watch the flames. They make pictures and dance around the logs."

"Granny used to have a real fire and there was always a cat curled up on the hearth and a kettle on the hob."

Karen and Henry had inherited their Granny's house. The old kitchen range in the living room had already been replaced with a tiled fireplace as Granny no longer was able to keep the range up to its glistening black surface with shining steel hinges on the oven door and edges of the hob and ash pan.

When Karen and Henry took their inheritance as their home, Henry filled in the opening to the grate in the living room, and had central heating installed.

On hearing the call, "Table for six," the group of friends moved into the dining room. Thoughts of fires and past times cast aside they sat down to plates of the famous Drake and Drummer hotpot.

A week later Karen and her friend Sylvia set off on a girls day out to the big town. An expedition of some importance was planned - clothes shops, shoe shops and a chance to be enveloped by the noises, smells and sights of a busy town.

On that day Henry, a teacher at the village school, waved his class of children goodbye and set off to walk home.

As he passed the village shop he stopped and gave thought to what was for tea. "I wonder if I can find something special for tea," he said out loud and stared into the shop. Unable to think of anything he set off home considering in his mind what the garden might have to offer.

As he walked up the path to the front door he thought, "Maybe some raspberries if any are ripe."

Inside the house Marmalade, the ginger tomcat, lay on the hearth rug.

Henry gave Marmalade a gentle tickle behind the ears, opened the window and set to making some coffee.

Sitting in the living room, Henry's mind wandered as he looked at the enclosed fire place. Memories came back to his childhood when there was an open fire in the kitchen range of his parent's house.

"It's true," he said looking at Marmalade. "There are pictures in the flames."

Suddenly he sat up straight. "That's it. I'll give Karen a surprise. I'll take that covering off the grate and have a fire burning when she comes home. We can both sit and look at the flames dancing."

A quick hunt around the garage produced some kindling. Paper and matches he found in the kitchen. "I'll need some coal," he said to himself. With a quick trip back to the village shop in the car, the bag of coal was purchased and driven home.

Having checked the time the bus carrying Karen was due back from the town, Henry assembled the materials necessary for a fire and settled down to read the newspaper, smiling.

He went over the plan again in his mind.

Pick some raspberries.

Cut some flowers. Place in vase of water on window sill. Leave window open for Marmalade.

Assemble paper, kindling, matches, coal.

Bus due in village six pm so light fire about five-twenty pm.

Action time duly arrived.

Henry duly applied a match to some crumpled newspaper, and placed a handful of kindling on the blaze. A small trail of smoke went up the chimney.

"That doesn't seem to be working very well," muttered Henry.

Suddenly he remembered that if the fire was slow burning his mother used to push a bunch of burning paper up the chimney.

He pushed a large bunch of paper up the chimney, applied a light to it and stepped back. A trickle of soot fell down the front of the burning paper. Suddenly there came a roaring noise, more soot fell down onto the hearth and the roaring increased.

Marmalade awoke, rushed over the settee onto the window ledge and, knocking the flower vase over, shot out through the window.

More soot dropped down the chimney, and to Henry's puzzlement there were some glowing embers falling onto the hearth.

Outside in the next-door garden there was a scream of horror. Mrs. Smith's back garden was filling with a thick black smoke pushed along by a gentle wind.

Also in her garden spread over several lines, her weekly wash, - sheets, towels, clothing, - all was being fouled in smoke. Mrs. Smith's language was most unladylike and mostly unprintable. From the chimney of Henry's house there arose a plume of thick black smoke and - horror of horrors - flicks of flame.

Up on the hillside James Potts spotted a cloud of smoke arising from the village. Grabbing his mobile phone, he called 999 FIRE.

Sitting on the bus with her friend Sylvia, Karen was startled as a fire engine lights flashing and siren on passed them.

"What's going on?" The passengers looked at each other.

The fire engine was manned by a volunteer crew who had not previously experienced a chimney fire.

On getting off the bus Karen was alarmed to see the fire engine outside her house and a fireman on the roof with a hose which he was using to direct water down the chimney.

Staggering to the open front door Karen choked over a tarry smell and found her living room walls stained and a soaking wet carpet.

She fainted.

The firemen soon had the blaze under control and Karen, having recovered her senses, surveyed her living room with horror. Henry was a shivering wreck who cowered behind the sofa as Karen threw ruined pictures and ornaments at him.

In due course the insurance claim for the damage done to the house was settled and Karen did not divorce Henry as she had threatened. She accepted his intentions had been good.

Henry's mother gave her son a carved notice to hang over the fireplace when it was repaired.

*"BEWARE THE ROAD TO HELL. IT IS PAVED WITH GOOD INTENTIONS"*

# Amanda Lovejoy

## Where Am I?

### About Amanda Lovejoy

A thalassophile, ( I looked that up too) rapidly becoming Scottish by osmosis.
Lover of everything nano: science geek, matter of fact.
Aim in life : to stop the world and get off. The human race is exhausting.
Word collector who likes to spend words like the wind, a sailor on shore leave. Any language is good. Favourite word "granny".
Brain analyst. Still working on that one...
Artist : sees the world in vivid colour even on a grey day.
Gardener, a mother/ nurture thing. I blame my mother
Chef. I'll relax in any kitchen. Don't let me in if you are covetous.
Retired teacher and lecturer. Learning is powerful. Once on that surf wave it takes you flying off.
Unrelenting, Creative mind. Who needs sleep? (Me)
In my "right mind"

Would like to force children to write left-handed
Want to ban plastic crap stuck on kids comics.
What message does it send to children?
Protester with small "p"
Not old enough to write a letter to the newspapers
yet.

Leave me in a meadow with the insects* and
wildflowers and I will be happy for evermore
...as long as there aren't any cows. Sitting
about scheming the human downfall by global
warming. Maybe God is female and she was
thinking of cheese when she created them? Fair
enough.

*not clegs. Now fruit flies (in my kitchen) you can talk
to, but clegs won't listen to reason. They just bite! Such
is life in West Scotland.

# Where Am I?

The rain had stopped and it wasn't nearly so windy. The air still and cold. Early April. I had followed the road around the island. Dipping in and out, following the contours of the coastline. For what else does one do on a small island but see what is at the other end? A perfect, smooth road by our Isle of Arran standards, but 200 miles away. A single track with passing bays always in sight. Few cars with a friendly wave from every driver as we danced in and out. I drove clockwise, they anti- clockwise. I as slowly as I could to take in the scenery ; the rugged, rocky landscape, the promising machair and views of white beaches. But how to get to them?

I had checked the time of the tides and was now going where the road took me. Trying to find somewhere to stop that wasn't a passing bay, I pulled over on a verge, high up over an isthmus. Before me a big, empty, round bay. Not as beautiful as the beaches I wanted to reach on my way. This looked as if a plasterer had taken their trowel and smoothed over the wet sand except the edges. The sea was out in the far distance.

I thought of all the people that might have stood on this spot. Bronze age settlers looking for flint washed up on the shore. Norsemen beaching their boats, but not staying long. Desperate, hungry people collecting cockles during the potato famine.

Now I looked and contemplated, the rough edges of the beach studded with plastic litter blown across the Atlantic, bringing me back to the 21st century.

And in the distance a wind sock danced, bright scarlet

Lost in thought when suddenly it went dark! Behind me a loud noise and something huge and grey screamed inches above my head. An aeroplane! Racing towards the wind sock, dipping down onto the sand like a damselfly. This was the daily passenger flight from Glasgow.

By the time I drove to the other end of the beach to the wee airport, a dozen people were descending the steps of the plane, some looking rather shaken and nearly as white as the beach. There we spectators stood and watched, excited children, me and a couple of mildly interested sheep.

*Caution: Beware of sand blast during aircraft movements.*
*Tràigh Mhor (Big Beach), Isle of Barra.*

# Barb Taub

## Top Ten Reasons Not to Get Married (For Women) ° How Barb and I Ended Up in the Castle by Peri Taub, PTWP

### About Barb Taub

BARB TAUB is a humor and urban fantasy author, caffeinated AussieDog wrangler, Yankee expat, and travel junkie. Following her daring daytime escape to England, Barb has lived in a medieval castle, a Hobbit House, and a magic Scottish Isle. Most recently, her dog Peri has allowed Barb to transcribe her memoirs. You can find Barb online at https://barbtaub.com/

# Top Ten Reasons Not to Get Married (For Women)

A while ago several of my friends were discussing the number of wedding presents to be purchased this time of year. Somehow (there may have been margaritas involved) the topic turned to things somebody should have mentioned before the I-do's.

My fellow women, many brave margaritas were sacrificed to bring you the cautionary warnings in the following list.

**If you get married, chances are good your spouse will be a male_____** [*fill in blank from list below. Bonus points if you get all ten.*]**

**10. DRIVER:** Unless you live in Manhattan or have accumulated buckets of disposable income the old-fashioned way (lottery, inheritance, sneaking onto a city bus that's had an accident so you can claim a back injury), sooner or later you and your husband will find yourselves in the same vehicle without benefit of professional chauffeur. My theory is that there is a boys-only supplemental drivers-ed class that the girls never see. There (in addition to the cabal hand-signal involving middle fingers) boys learn the sacred tenets of manly driving:

- A man never asks for directions. *GPS/SatNav Corollary*: A man is sure he knows a better route than the satellite directions. He also knows a better route than the Uber driver, and any taxi driver worldwide who hasn't passed the London cabbies' Knowledge test.

- If a woman drives a car belonging to a man who is not suffering from at least two broken limbs (casts are helpful here), other male drivers are required to question his masculinity.

- When a woman is driving, a man knows the importance of pointing out every car, fence, pedestrian, and potential hazard in a three-county region. He also knows she will be grateful. Eventually.

- Under no circumstances will a man make more than one potty stop per trip. That's what God made empty Coke bottles for.

**9. HOARDER**: Your husband will know that if anything happens to his good old college sweatshirt covered in his good old college stains, he will never be able to exercise again. Also, the second you throw away that take-out container with the cure for cancer he's been culturing in the back of the fridge, it will trigger the immediate meltdown of polar icecaps. As you sit on your roof, waters rising around you, he'll be forced to point out that it's all your fault. If only you hadn't tossed that leftover Kung Pao Chicken, you could have held out until help arrives. And if only you hadn't gotten rid of that special sweatshirt he needed for his workout routine, he would be in good enough physical shape to turn the rowing machine and one of the bathtubs into a rescue boat. If only.

**8. LAUNDRY**: Bad case scenario–he might expect you to do his laundry. Even worse case scenario– he will do your laundry.

**7. FEMALE SYMPATHIZER WANNABE**: Take your average millennial husband. He knows that PMS is out there, his enemy, waiting to turn a relatively rational wife into someone whose reply to "Hello," is "What do you mean by that, you Neanderthal?" He also knows that even to suggest, "That time of the month?" and he could be on sofa-sentry until sometime next century. If he's lucky. Will this stop him from asking, "Touch of the old hormones?" Of course it won't. (But it might help your defense when you're trying to get the homicide charges reduced to involuntary manslaughter...)

**6. BODILY FLUID REJECTOR**. (No, I didn't mean *those* bodily fluids. Get your mind out of the gutter, woman...) Men, for the most part, cannot clean up vomit. That's why they go far, far away for spring break and guys' weekends. Because what's upchucked in Vegas gets cleaned up in Vegas–by someone else. So be prepared, ladies: if you get married, your child will not cough, blow, wipe, or barf on anyone but you.

**5. GUILT SPREADER**: Your mother-in-law might be the Travel Agent of the Year on the Grandparent Guilt Trip Express. But read the fine print before you start shopping for that Blue Almonds Moses Basket. It starts with the episiotomy, and next thing you know your single-digit clothing size, ability to stand without swaying an invisible child on your hip, or to speak in full sentences is gone. Suddenly your kids get all the good lines, while you open your mouth and out comes your mother. It really puts owning a cat into perspective.

**4. PHOTOGRAPHER**: Husbands have strange ideas about what makes the perfect photo. He will look through a camera's viewfinder and take the shot *even if it does not contain a single child or close relative.* If forced to photograph members of your immediate family, he will spend so long waiting for all eyes to open and all fingers to be removed from bodily orifices that the children will have grown two sizes and wandered into another zip code before the shutter clicks. Thanks to the freedom of digital cameras and phones with exceptionally large SD cards, most women know you should click the shutter nonstop on the off-chance that a child you are related to will wander past the viewfinder. A little photoshop magic and voila! Perfect shot.

**3. PERSONAL HYGIENE INNOVATOR**: How do men know these things? Is it possible that some mother gathers her little males and tells them, "Boys, your wife will need reminders that there is a man around the house, so be sure to leave the toilet seat raised, the manly underwear on the heater, and your personal athletic gear looped over the towel rack. Oh, and come out and talk to her while you're flossing your teeth. Wives love that."

**2. LITTLE HELPER**: Many husbands see marriage as a partnership. They're willing to do their fair share–as long as it's not anything that has to be done at a defined time, or where their hands get wet. Or if it involves bodily fluids of course. (*see #6 above*) For example, with encouragement he will ~~clean the kitchen, clear the table, load the dishwasher,~~ rearrange the dirty dishes on the counter. When it comes to cooking, he'll ~~willingly peel vegetables, cut up dead chickens, chop the onions, and~~ pierce the film. Luckily, he knows the

Kitchen Fairy will handle the rest. You didn't know about the Kitchen Fairy? Her little sister, the Bathroom Fairy, is the one who replaces toilet paper on the spindle. She also knows the magic spell to make the vacuum turn on.

The top reason not to get married?

### 1. YOU'RE ALREADY PLAYING HOUSE.

*Our grandmothers:* "Why would a man buy an entire cow when milk is so cheap?

*Our daughters:* "Well, why would a woman buy an entire pig for 4 1/2 inches of sausage?"

*\*\*The funny thing about this list? It contains all but one of the ten top reasons FOR men to get married.*

Editorial Note from Barb: Of course, marriage is a crap-shoot where the odds are all against you. But I took that bet over forty years ago, and I've been winning ever since. You can too. (Except for the part where he helps with your laundry. Don't go there.)

# How Barb and I Ended Up in the Castle — by Peri Taub, PTWP* (Pandemic Therapist With Paws)

*\*As transcribed by her person, Barb Taub, whose opposable thumbs might as well be useful for something besides opening dog food...*

When Barb told me some people get depressed as their last child leaves for college, my ears perked up. This was clearly a job for the Therapist Dog. Although I was still a fairly new therapist, I knew what had to be done. I lifted one ear, tilted my head to the side, and raised one paw. How does that make you feel, Barb?

"I'm torn." She looked around the (clean) living room, and eyed the remote, in plain sight exactly where it belonged.

I rubbed my chin across her leg. *Homework!*

Barb sighed, but I'd already trained her well. She pulled out a piece of paper and drew a line down the middle. In the first column she wrote:

EMPTY NEST: PROS

1. Everything stays right where I left it.

2. I don't have to put on clothes.

3. The Hub and I could get drunk and have sex anywhere in the house. Anytime.

4. I don't have a sullen, moody roommate who avoids me except for fleeting moments when affection is permitted, never cleans up her own mess, stays out until all hours without once checking in, but still expects to find food waiting at her preferred hours.

Barb chewed the top of her pencil thoughtfully before starting on the CONS column. After careful consideration, she moved #3 to the CONS column. After further thought, she moved #4 to CONS with a note: *Actually, we still have the cat.*

I know from talking to the other dogs, that some empty-nesting parents turn the kids' rooms into a craft room or he-den. Barb and the Hub put the house up for sale, forwarded the mail, and we moved to England.

At first I wasn't worried about the move. I'd never been on a long plane ride, but I've always loved traveling as long as Barb was there. It was actually fine. Until it wasn't. I had to go into a kennel with the door fastened shut. But the worst part was that Barb had to leave. My kennel was loaded into a special room on the plane along with other kennels. Nobody in any of them was happy about it.

But then it got so much worse. After we landed, I was sent to Heathrow Airport's pet jail. It was hours before I heard Barb's voice on the other side of the door. Finally! But wait... she was crying. Begging. I tried to get out of the kennel. *Curse you, evolution, for my lack of opposable thumbs.*

Eventually, Barb's voice was gone. I couldn't believe it. She'd left me in a foreign country. My kennel was loaded onto a truck and we drove for hours to someplace called Leeds, which apparently is home to Dog Prison. All around me dogs were howling and crying. They took away my kennel and even my special blanket that Barb had rubbed against her armpits so it would smell right.

I was lying on the prison-issued dog bed, which was plastic but at least better than the concrete floor, when the Bad Thing happened. At first it was just a feeling, a sense that something was wrong. Next thing I knew, I was slammed down on the floor, shaking so hard my teeth rattled. When I came to, I couldn't quite remember what had happened. My eyes didn't work, it was hard to stand up or walk, and I was smell-blind. Worst of all, I'd had an accident, a bad one, and it was all over me. I was a bad dog.

The jailers sprayed me down and hosed out my cell. It was cold and I was still shaking, but I didn't care because I knew what had happened. I was in jail for being a bad dog, and the

Bad Thing was my punishment.

The other dogs didn't know how long we'd been at the jail. No surprise there. We're dogs: object permanence isn't really our thing. (We only have NOW and NOT-NOW, or if you're a Labrador, EAT and WAITING-TO-EAT.) But finally, Barb did come. She told me there had been a mix-up with the paperwork, and I was sentenced to quarantine in Dog Prison until she could work things out. She cried some more and told me she would come back and visit every week until they let me go. She brought me my bed and second-favorite blanket that she must have done the armpit thing on because it smelled right, and a bunch of my toys. But best of all, she told me I was a good dog.

I was deliriously happy to finally leave prison behind. Sadly, the Bad Thing must have followed us. The first time it attacked me, Barb and the Hub raced to the emergency vet on duty in the next village. Jeremy was kind of hard to understand – Barb said he was French – but he and Barb started talking about canine epilepsy. Apparently, that was Bad-Thing's name. And it was here to stay. In the years to come, the Bad Thing showed up many times, but it was never as bad as the first time in Doggie Prison. Because, no matter how often the Bad Thing came, Barb still said I was a good dog. Even if she then took me into the Dog Drowning Room and gave me a bath.

▼ ( ˊ ̇ ˋ ) ▼

As with most of Barb's important life decisions, moving into the castle was an accident. When the Hub started his job in the north of England, Barb was sure we would live in a cottage named something like Rose Cottage of Upper Long Chipping at Little Buttsfield. I would have a charming basket on the floor next to the Aga, and we'd all drink tea from pots covered by adorable knitted sweaters. Even though we're Americans, we would drink that tea with milk, and we'd actually like it that way.

What became clear as Barb and I went from one estate agent to another was that – even if there had been such a thing as a multiple listing service in England – there was no Rose

Cottage.

*[NOTE from Barb: True, actually. Even the massed might and deep purses of Hollywood location shoppers failed to turn up a single instance of Kate Winslet's perfect English cottage for the movie The Holiday, so they built her Rosehill Cottage from chicken wire and fiberglass. But I could tell it wasn't a real English cottage, because there was no sign of a dog or a cat, or even an emergency backup hedgehog.]*

To take their minds off the fact that we'd be cottageless for the foreseeable future, I decided to take Barb and the Hub out for a drive. We turned up a country lane and drove until it ended in front of a lovely house. The owner came running out to see why we were trespassing on his (who has one a half-mile long?) driveway. When he realized we were a pair of clueless Americans with an adorable dog, he took us to a pub (England being a long-civilized country, dogs are welcome in pubs), described the best places to live locally, and finished by writing down the names of some villages for us to check out.

We drove to the first one, turned a corner, and stopped dead. In front of us, massive stone towers soared up to crenelated battlements above an enormous gate with a smaller human-sized door. Basically, we were gawping up at an honest-to-Ivanhoe gigantic stone castle. There's a great word I learned in England – gobsmacked*.

*[I think it means two Americans and one dog staring in shock, whilst – you get to say whilst here – whimpering weak WTF?s.]*

I was expecting someone to pop out the little door and tell us, "Nobody can see the wizard. Not nobody, not no-how!" Instead, a lady came through the portcullis* and – as required by ancient English law which makes it illegal to speak to a stranger or really even a friend in public without the presence of a dog, horse, or weather event – she stopped to fuss my ears.

> *[Portcullis is another great British word that means honking huge stone arch with spiky gates where Robin Hood cuts the rope so it drops down to block the sheriff's evil henchmen. I'm pretty sure.]

The lady looked up from petting me and admitted to Barb and the Hub that it was her family's castle. She told us they occasionally rented parts of it, although nothing was currently available. Out of pity or because she thought it was the only way to get rid of us, the lady accepted our email address. By an amazing miracle, she contacted us a few days later to say long-term residents were unexpectedly moving out, so one of the corner towers would be available if we were still interested.

*Would Americans be interested in living in an actual castle?* I think that's the poster-child for rhetorical questions. We moved in immediately.

If you've ever lived in a tiny village in England, you will not be nearly as surprised as Barb and I were at what happened our first day of castle residency. If you've been living in Seattle (where the Seattle Freeze = super friendly but never friends) you might even be a little scared. We emerged through the portcullis for my morning constitutional, Barb still wearing what she'd worn to bed. This consisted, basically, of almost every item of clothing she owned, and she was still moaning that she'd never experienced cold like the inside of a medieval castle with four-foot thick stone walls.

We were immediately tagged as fresh blood, captured, and marched over to Village Coffee Morning in the Victorian-era Village Hall. There may be some places where Village Coffee Morning is a casual event. I just don't think those places are in England. Certainly not in our little village, where the weekly caffeination was the place major decisions, changes, and explanations of village life were enacted over coffee and of course, a few raffle ticket sales. Everyone there told Barb I was adorable (which didn't surprise her) and slipped me clandestine treats (which didn't disappoint me).

Village Coffee was also where Barb learned to speak British. For example, at one Coffee Morning early on, Barb described her reaction to finding the side of her car bashed in. "I was so pissed off," she said. "And as the day went on, I just got more and more pissed. In fact, by that night, I couldn't even remember the last time I'd been so totally pissed."

You could have cut the collective silence that followed with a knife. Finally, one of our new friends asked if Barb knew *pissed* means drunk. All nodded sagely, and the discussion turned to the shame one felt to run out of homemade jam and have to serve (her voice lowered) *jam from a shop*.

A few weeks after our first coffee morning, Barb got a phone call from someone who introduced himself as her partner* for hosting Coffee Morning the next day, and did she prefer to bring the biscuits or the scones? (More gobsmackage...) Since our American impression of scones was triangular-shaped pastries with the weight and often the flavor of hockey pucks, Barb agreed to bring something else. Something charming. Something American. Something she could actually cook.

*[Public Service Announcement which Barb totally missed: IF YOU ATTEND VILLAGE COFFEE MORE THAN ONCE, YOUR NAME WILL APPEAR IN THE PARISH NEWSLETTER AND YOU'LL BE ON THE COFFEE-ROTA, RESPONSIBLE FOR SERVING COFFEE AND SCONES ONCE A MONTH. FOR THE REST OF YOUR NATURAL LIFE. YOU'VE BEEN WARNED.]

Thus began Barb's Coffee Morning career of mystifying our neighbors with weird American foods. First up were the cupcakes ("Your fairy cakes are too big and wear far too much icing," she was informed). Next was the blueberry coffeecake, which nobody touched until Barb explained it wasn't really made out of coffee. Most disconcerting of all was the strange foreign food item Barb told them was called... a bagel. Nobody had ever eaten one before, although a few admitted to hearing of them. They gathered around and stared as she suggested they top their bagels with cream cheese.

"She means Philadelphia," someone explained. "In America they think it's called cream cheese."

Undeterred, Barb unveiled our *pièce de résistance*. "Lox!"

Silence.

"Here in England," one lady finally told Barb kindly, "...we call that salmon."

Many looked frankly skeptical as Barb sliced bagels. "Is it an American donut?"

"They eat fish on their donuts in America then?"

"Do you have any homemade jam for that?"

After that, Barb mostly brought brownies on our assigned coffee morning day.

# Tom Kelly

## THE BIKE ° BEACHES

### About Tom Kelly

Tom has lived on Arran for the past five years, after a career in public service. He fell in love with his wife Alison, who first brought him to Arran, where he fell in love with it also. They were married a short distance from where they now live. They have three children, one of whom now lives on the island. As well as writing for pleasure, he enjoys contract bridge, walking, and sailing on the bay outside his home.

# The Bike

Gerry stood back, waiting for her friend and surveying the passing crowds of holiday makers ebbing and flowing along the promenade. She looked up at the bronze statue of Britannia atop her granite plinth looking across Troon Bay towards Arran. The war memorial seemed out of place on this joyous summer day as families and friends engaged in the simple pleasures of being on holiday. Looking at her watch, Gerry acknowledged that she was early, but remained slightly anxious in the midst of all these strangers. Fashion conscious, she distracted herself by looking at what the visitors were wearing, comparing her summer attire with theirs. She felt smart enough, but strangely out of touch with the crowd in her shorts and Breton tee shirt. This subsided as she spotted Maggie approaching.

Maggie's red hair bobbed in and out of the masses as she made her way. She was small in stature compared to Gerry, but she always exuded confidence and enthusiasm in whatever she did. Today, thankfully, she wore a similar tee shirt design to her taller best pal, whose feeling of self-consciousness was immediately relieved.

Greetings and hugs completed, they surveyed the crowded beach and listened to the chatter of the west coast Scots and the occasional interlude of French, Italian and the other tongues of the foreign visitors brought here by the relaxed travel restrictions.

"What do you fancy doing Maggie?" Gerry enquired, squinting in the bright sunlight.

Maggie looked around in reply. "I'm not too sure. The beach will be roasting and I have only got my thin sandals on."

Gerry nodded, acknowledging the point being made. "You are right. I don't fancy working my way through those hordes either."

Maggie considered for a moment, "I'm a bit bored with going towards the Marine Hotel. Do you fancy going the other way to the Ballast Bank for a change?"

"Good idea."

A confirming nod all round and the two set off, negotiating the walkers in their familial groups, avoiding spilt ice creams and the swirling sand devils occasionally stirred by the light breeze. As they walked they overhead the compliments being paid to their town. "I never knew this place was on our doorstep. This is better than Spain and the food is better too," were not uncommon sentiments expressed by the visitors.

Gerry smiled, proud of her birthplace. "This is what it was like every summer in the old days, I suppose."

"My grandparents brought our family here on holiday from Glasgow every summer and that's how I ended up here," reflected Maggie. "I've got say it does bring some life back to the old place."

The crowds thinned as they left the amusements, ice cream and burger stall with its associated smells and temporary clientele. The term Scottish Riviera had seldom been used since the package deals of the late sixties had stolen the holiday makers away to foreign climes. But this year, the sunshine and the release from the pandemic lockdown combined to bring the crowds back with a vengeance.

"Is that where the Caldwell's used to live?" asked Maggie as they passed a familiar row of houses.

"Yes, in the top flat" Gerry replied, "They moved to Stirling. John was my big brother's best pal and I think he still misses him."

"I can just imagine," replied Maggie, "the carry on's they boys got up to."

Gerry still looked up to her big brother, recognising his lead in signposting her life. He often took the brunt of their parent's criticisms, but he had been the first of the family to go to university. She was proud of him, despite the usual sibling bickering.

"You are right, there." mused Gerry. "Did I tell you about the time John got given a camera? He had Ian and their gang posing and doing all kinds of stupid things like pulling faces and doing somersaults off the sea wall. Mind you, John had to make a run for it when he told them that next time he used the camera he would put some film in it."

Maggie giggled as she pictured the scene, before chipping in with her own recollection.

"Those two got up to some really crazy capers. My brother once told me about them all going over to Arran with the Boys Brigade for a camping weekend. My brother went officially with the troop, but Ian and John were now overaged. When it came to the camp they had assumed that they would be able to pitch in with their pals in one of the tents. However, the leaders told them to clear off, as they were not wanting to take any responsibility for them being there. I understand they ended up spending the night in a bus shelter in the middle of a storm. Sleepless, bedraggled, cold and starving before they made their way home on the first ferry."

Gerry snorted, "You are asking me if I remember! I have never seen such a row. Ian got a right good blasting from our Ma, as she chased him around the kitchen with a broom." They both laughed out loud at the memory, just as the Ballast Bank came into view.

In the distance the Ballast Bank rose up like Ayers Rock, standing proud from the otherwise flat ground surrounding it with the trademark steep accent to a flat summit stretching to the equally steep descent. The image of the Australian outback was enhanced further by the long drought of the summer that had weathered the grass into something brown and strange and alien. There the connection to Ayer's Rock ended. The  Ballast Bank was no freak of nature. It was the result of mankind's industry; a site where in times past sailing ships deposited worthless sand and earth in return for the rich coal from the Ayrshire mines.

Suddenly they both stopped dead in their tracks.

"What on earth is that!" exclaimed Gerry, "What have they done to the paddling pool? It's gone."

They looked at each other dumbfounded. As toddlers they had enjoyed paddling in the icy cold water. A safe alternative to when the sea was inclement or to the risks of being stung by the seasonal jellyfish. Most toddlers in the town had been baptised onto the first rung of the "learning to swim ladder" here at this pool. It was a rite of passage common to the young people of the town.

Their annoyance at the disappearance of the pool was ameliorated to some degree by their curiosity at what now unfolded in front of them. "What are those things?" asked Gerry looking at a collection of unusual machines covered mainly in plastic and bright yellow warning tape.

Maggie studied the scene before replying with a note of authority. "I think it is one of the Council's ideas to keep everyone fit." She knew about the importance of being healthy through her family's long-standing patronage of the Marine's leisure centre. They approached with some curiosity and increasing excitement.

The workman with the bright orange council tabard had his back to them as they approached. Kneeling, he finished applying the last of the mortar securing a piece of equipment to the ground.

"Excuse me, but what is that?" enquired Gerry.

The workman rose up and turned with a smile of pleasure that his labours had been noticed. He looked at the object obscured in its wrapping  and aimed at  preventing imminent use.

"Hello ladies.  A fine day to you." He addressed them with a mixture of flattery and possibly a hint of amusement. Mopping his brow with a rag, he returned his attention to the object in question. Taking pride in his work and pleased at his contribution to its existence, he pondered the question before addressing Gerry, "I am not quite sure what its proper name is, but it is to keep us all fit and healthy."

At this point, Maggie came to the fore. "Told you so, I was right, it is about keeping you fit. This is all about kin...es... kines... kinesthetics'!" stumbling to find the unfamiliar word, before successfully spitting it out. "My Father told me about this. It was invented or something for submariners during the war. It's to do with keeping your muscles working when you are in a confined space."

The workman smiled and confirmed Maggie's statement. "I think you are probably right. This machine will help people to exercise their leg muscles by stretching them against varying weights, because nobody walks anymore. Too busy using their cars to go around the corner to the shops and such". And then, rather saucily, he remarked "Mind you, I can see you won't need it much as you both have very nice legs". Gerry snorted dismissively at this overfamiliarity, albeit with a modicum of delight at the intended compliment. Maggie just gave him a look that said it all.

Gerry was first to ask, "Can we have a shot?"

"Not on this one" replied the Workman "the official opening is not until next week". Then rubbing his chin and turning to consider some of his earlier work he reviewed Gerry's request... "The cement is still drying on most of them hence the warning signs, but I put the bike over there in first and it should now be safe to use."

He led them to one of the other machines and carefully unravelled the warning tape and unfolded the plastic covering to reveal a brand-new bike, albeit one without wheels.

Maggie put her hands on her hips and laughed, "Well nobody is going to steal this to go around the corner for a pint of milk. It's well secured. I'll go first."

Maggie moved to get onto the bike, but hindered by her lack of height, she found it difficult to get her leg over the saddle. She considered the task with new resolve, cocked her leg in an attempt to loosen up her hip, and had a go at touching her toes as she prepared for a second attempt. "Let me have another shot at this." Again, Maggie's effort was to no avail. She was pitifully short of the target.

The workman stepped forward with clasped hands, "Do you want a leg up?"

Instantly the universal parental message drummed into every child from an early age came to the fore; never take offers of sweets from strangers and that includes "leg ups" that went way beyond the boundary of proper behaviour in Maggie's view. Hastily, she declined the offer with a blunt "No thank **YOU** very much!" and stepped back from the fray. Meanwhile, Gerry took an interest and approached the bike; surveyed it and then in one balletic swing of her leg perched herself on the saddle.

"**Wow!**" gulped the workman and Maggie in unison.

Basking in the pleasant surprise and glory of her newly discovered agility, Gerry enquired. "Now, what do I do?"

Duh!" snorted the Workman, "You pedal it of course."

Gerry located the pedals, but strained to turn them.

"Put your back into it, lass." shouted Maggie in support.

Gerry stood up on the pedals to exert her full weight, but with no success. "They're definitely stuck!" she exclaimed, "I think it's broken".

The workman quizzically approached and pushed down at the intransigent pedal, before stepping back and reviewing the bike. He indicated that Gerry should take a rest. He rubbed his chin in thought, "Wait a second... its adjustable." He stooped to turn a knob on the handlebar. "Now try."

Gerry stood up and balanced on the pedals in readiness.

"Go on" urged Maggie.

Gerry steadied herself, before applying maximum force to the task. She lurched forward as her over-zealous push on the pedal met absolutely no resistance. The old adage about pride coming before a fall was never more appropriate, as the pedals whizzed out of all control. Toppling forward her glow of pride had swiftly been replaced by her cold, pale fear of falling off. Desperately regaining the saddle, "Stop it" she screamed. "Let me off!" She took her feet off the pedals and stretched out her legs, a parody of going down a steep hill. The pedals immediately took on a life of their own, seemingly increasing speed as they realised their unbridled freedom.

Again, the workman came to the rescue, reaching out to restore her balance. "Wait, let me put some tension on the pedals before you get off. I can't afford for you to hurt yourself. It's more than my jobs worth." he muttered. He readjusted the knob and assisted her down. Tearfully, Gerry straightened herself as she tried to regain her dignity.

Maggie's heartfelt hug of support was warmly received. "There, there. You certainly did better than me." she comforted.

"I'm really sorry!" The workman's face held genuine remorse and relief that Gerry was not physically hurt. "I hadn't realised I had taken off all the tension when I released the pedals." He looked at the bike and readjusted the knob slightly to increase the pedal tension. He wanted to make it up to Gerry in the unlikely event she should want to try again. "Hey, there's a saddle adjustment too, so that you can lower it." He beckoned to Maggie. "Do you want another shot at it?"

Wide eyed and scowling, Maggie's grimace of incredulity said it all before confirming her reply. "Not on your Nelly, thank you very much," she retorted. "I think that is enough for one day, don't you Gerry?"

"Too damn right. That's definitely not something I am going to do again." Gerry nodded in agreement, rubbing her backside,as they both turned and left. "I'm ready for coffee and cake at the Marine now."

Maggie nodded "Maybe something stronger after all that."

The workman let out his breath, relieved nothing serious had come to pass. He then smiled to himself as he rewrapped the plastic and warning tape over the bike. He looked at the two figures as they slowly disappeared arm in arm and slightly bent double as they merged back into the crowd. With a small gasp of astonishment, he shook his head. A smile broke out on his  weathered face, a mixture of admiration and wonder. "God love them. I only hope I have half as much spark and energy as those two have when I get to their age. Eighty, if a day!"

# Beaches

The child Hussein noble stood, surveying the beach. This shore, was his land.
Sun blazing on this skeleton coast, the shimmering ocean beyond the white sand.
What future he pondered was beyond his fathom, horizons outside his scope.
Behind him camels silently came into view, bearing men ruthless with tethering rope.
The young man hopeless sat on a stony beach, watching his children playing.
Waves and thoughts in turmoil lashing the rocks. For the truth he was raving.
What future in this land of sanctuary? Hero or villain? Hold in the truth, stay illicit.
Justice blind. Tell no one, stay silent. My children, their future lost; remain complicit.
The old man stood broken, surveying the weed strewn beach overlooking the firth.
The land beyond lay hidden by cold mizzled grey, this so different from that of his birth.
The tide rolled in like the lines of a poem; in and out, endlessly ebb and flowing.
What could have been if not to a life enslaved, his kith and kin not knowing.
He pondered looking out on the life he lost through the fickleness of one's fate.
The scientist of his day, or even an Olympian, if only on a bone-laden beach, an hour late.

*Dedicated to all children still stolen into modern day slavery, in particular to Hussein, whom we know as Mo.*

**A gift from christine**

*Saw this and thought of you. Enjoy xx*
*From christine*

Gift note included with The Wife, The Mistress, and the Guinea Pig; & Other Stories

# Elizabeth Ross

## THE WEE HOUSE ° GETTING OLDER ° REVELATION ° THE WINDS THAT BLOW

### About Elizabeth Ross

Elizabeth is in retirement from a career in Pharmacy and exploring her creativity. She is married with a son and daughter and two granddaughters. She takes inspiration from the community, land and seascapes of the Isle of Arran for writing prose, poetry and music, and designing and crafting works in crochet and embroidery.

# The Wee House

## *1* *832*

The black cat crept warily out of the bushes and surveyed the house. Was it safe to come out and hunt in the long grass which it knew to be full of small, eatable creatures? Its instincts said, "Nobody watching" and it darted into a particularly favoured, overgrown patch where rich pickings of voles were to be found.

Flora, the human resident, was watching, saw the cat and smiled to herself. She knew it was feral, just like its ancestors. And like her house, they had been present since the village first began. They kept the vermin down and it was comforting to know that some things never changed. Her husband had been killed in an accident on the farm where, along with most of the other residents of their small hamlet, he had worked. Although the house was somewhat tumbledown, she felt lucky to have been gifted the cottage as recompense by a generous landlord, also near death in the big house on the hill. And even luckier to have escaped the constant belittling and bullying of an overbearing husband. With the cats, her cottage, and her son, and friends in Garthwaite, she was content.

The cats of the village were of a special strain, nearly always born black as soot, occasionally with a little white patch somewhere on their sleek, well-fed bodies. The farming community had plenty of grain stores where prey lived and the felines worked for their comfortable living. Generations of one family of such useful companions had been born, hunted and bred in the grounds of The Wee House. Its situation, a little set back from the lane and down a slight slope, gave it advantages in cover and opportunity for hunting. In later, more leisured times, its bucolic charm was considered to be most attractive.

From time to time, a kitten would be born more adventurous than its siblings and wander off to see what was inside this building. One such had been scooped up by Flora and tamed, with milk, love and the warmth of the fire in the ever-glowing hearth. This was undoubtedly the boss cat with a name, Thomasina, and a privileged perch on the ledge of the little arched dormer in the roof over the front door. As she sunned herself, Thomasina would lazily survey the larger dormers either side and beyond them the chimney stacks, one at each end, although only one was needed to warm the large open downstairs room.

Behind the cottage was a long slope leading down to the stream. This was the demesne of Thomasina who, whilst allowing other felines the lane-side ground at the front for hunting, kept this for herself. It was also Flora's favourite place, the warmth of the sun and the busy humming of the insects creating a haven of tranquillity and calm.

The hamlet was a collection of hovels accommodating the farm workers of the area. Farm work in the 1830s was labour intensive, families were large and a constant stream of potential labour was produced in the handful of dwellings grouped around the junction of two lanes. Water came from the local stream, each cottage had a garden for growing vegetables and a few chickens and they shared earth closets at the end of the plots.

Over the years, Flora's beloved cottage was passed down from mother to son to grandson and, with various repairs, kept out the weather for over a 100 years. And Thomasina's descendents, who regarded themselves as the real owners, continued through generations of all-black kittens to perform lookout duties on the windowsill.

### 1922

In 1922 the cottage was occupied by the widow's great granddaughter, Elsie. She was unmarried, reclusive and independent and, as the village had grown up around and beyond the road junction, her cottage had receded behind the ever-growing shrubs which hid her from curious eyes. Elsie's father had managed to save enough from his work as a railway clerk to create a small income for her and so, with her garden to sustain her, she needed little contact with the outside world. Occasionally she would go in the early morning to the village shop, greeting Martha, the shopkeeper, with a shy smile.

"Good morning, Martha. It's a beautiful day again isn't it?"

Martha would quietly close the door and turn the sign to 'closed'. "Yes. It's going to be another hot one. What would you like today, I have some fresh eggs in from the farm. Oh but I forgot, you have your own hens don't you?"

And so Elsie would buy her necessities and retreat once more into The Wee House.

The cats had grown with Elsie, one generation after another, and had developed into a strain of glossy black, watchful, independent creatures, who were particular as to the company they kept. Their presence persuaded the more superstitious villagers into wondering if Elsie might be a witch. They weren't quite sure but kept it in mind, especially around Hallowe'en. The cats still liked to climb on the roof and use the little dormer window ledge to sit and survey their feline kingdom. Intruding cats were hissed at, small rodents were spotted and marked as future prey and, as the aspect was southerly, the sun warmed their black fur in a most acceptable fashion.

Several children of the village passed the house on their way to school, and it was a game amongst the girls to see if they could spot a cat on The Wee House's roof. If so it was considered a lucky day and they would skip happily the rest of the way. The boys weren't so bothered about a cat; brawling, pushing and shoving each other was much more fun. But neither boys nor girls ever saw Elsie and didn't give any thought to who lived in the house and fed the cats. Most cats in the village were semi-feral, having to find their own meals as they had been doing for generations.

Then one day in late March 1922, a group of girls were on the way home from school when one of them, Jeannie, looking out for the cat, saw a hideous face pressed against the inside of the little dormer window.

"Aaagh, help. It's the witch." She screamed, and ran away.

Gertie and Florence shrieked loudly and ran hysterically down the lane after her.

"It's her, she'll get us. Come on, run." The three dashed away as fast as they could, dragging the smaller children with them.

On the following morning, the girls gathered at the lane end, none of them wanting to go by the house but having no other route to school. At last they plucked up the courage to creep past, ducking down below the level of the bushes until Gertie, taller than the rest, looked up and screamed. "It's there, the face," and they all ran down the lane crying hysterically.

At twenty-three, their town-bred teacher, Marianne Pendy, was not used to the ways of the country and had no idea of the depth of superstition in the locals. The chaos which reigned in school that day irritated her. The fire in the stove wouldn't burn properly and the pans of water set to boil wouldn't heat up. The rain beat against the windows leaking through every hole and crack, and Miss Pendy was struggling to keep control as the children chattered and wailed. The bigger boys took advantage of the turmoil to cause as much disruption as possible, scuffling with each other, pinching the girls and pulling their hair.

Most of the children went home for a mid-day bite but the ones that had to pass The Wee House refused to leave and their teacher didn't know what to do. She called for Jacob, the caretaker, a taciturn old man, retired from labouring who did little more than see to the coal supply for the stove. He muttered, " Ah take no notice of the little blighters. They saw Elsie in her window and thought she was coming after them."

At 4 o'clock, Marianne thankfully sent the children away home and sat down with a cup of tea to consider the situation. The children ran past the house as fast as they could without looking for a cat or anything else and as soon as they were home, threw themselves into their chores with a vigour never previously seen. Mothers were surprised but assumed the teacher was at last encouraging them to be useful rather than waste time on "Them fancy subjects, reeding, riting and 'rithmetic."

Easter was approaching and the vicar asked Marianne if the children would be in church for the Palm Sunday service. His flock were not reliable attenders, especially the young ones when the sun was out.

"Of course, I'll encourage them. If I go and collect pussy willow for them to carry in a church procession, it might interest a few more."

She went in search of pussy willow on the banks of the stream. It was a fine spring day and she wandered along, soaking up the warm sunshine and delighting in seeing early signs of foliage all around her. At a clump of willow trees she cut off some of the lower trailing twigs on which the pussy willows were just opening. Marianne lost track of the time, and she wandered further along until she saw a gap in the bushes. Curiosity drove her to squeeze through it and the sight stopped her in her tracks. An open space, almost surrounded by tall bushes, was covered in daffodils, some open, some just beginning to bend their heads. Amongst them, oblivious to her presence, was her grandmother bending over the flowers stroking and talking to them. Marianne was stunned into silence. She had been close to her grandmother and thought she was having an hallucination. Then she realised this was a real person dressed in her grandmother's style. She had been in the village nearly a year now, and thought she knew by sight all the inhabitants. But this woman she had never seen before. Her long skirt swept her ankles and a large woollen shawl was draped over her shoulders. When she straightened up, Marianne could take in her long dark hair with a striking white streak running back from her forehead, piercing blue eyes and the deep burgundy-coloured birthmark covering half her face.

The pair studied each other in surprised silence and then, eerily, a black cat appeared from the bushes and weaved itself round the older woman's legs. And before either of them could speak, it went to Marianne and did the same. In some confusion at the realisation that she was trespassing, she bent down and stroked it under its chin and along its back.

"Oh. So you like cats then?"

Marianne jerked upright at the sound, a mellifluous voice with only a trace of the local accent.

"I do," she replied, "I've always loved them and miss not having my own."

She looked away from the woman in confusion as she realised that the person before her, although wearing old-fashioned clothes, was young, perhaps only ten years older than herself. As she looked up the slope she saw a small house at the top and after a moment of staring at it, realised it was the back of The Wee House.

"Oh my goodness. Is that your house and this is your garden? You must be the lady who ..." and Marianne's voice tailed off as she wondered what to say. "I'm the teacher and the children were a little restless the other day after they passed your house." She didn't know what else she could say for fear of upsetting the lady.

"I'm Elsie. They saw me looking out of the window and were scared. I'm so sorry, I love to see the children playing but they all run away from me because of this." She pointed to the birthmark. Marianne couldn't think of anything to say that wasn't trite and meaningless so she just smiled at the woman and continued to stroke the cat.

"You are not repulsed by me then? I see so few people I never know what they will do."

Marianne bent again to stroke the cat while she thought hard. Then she stood up straight, smiled at Elsie and said, "My name is Marianne. I have learned not to judge the contents of the parcel by the packaging. I'm sure your life is hard enough as it is without ignorant people making it harder. Now I'm sorry if I've disturbed you by trespassing. I was collecting pussy willow for the children to take to church at Easter so had better get on with it. It's been lovely meeting you, perhaps we can meet again sometime?"

"That would be so kind of you, I do get lonely. Could you come in this way again? Please."

And with that heartfelt plea, Elsie turned and walked briskly up the slope to the house.

Marianne stood and watched Elsie's departure, thinking furiously. No wonder the children were scared of her with that white streak in her long dark hair and the hideous birthmark. They were rural children of families long immersed in superstitions about the harvest and winter survival, and largely ignorant of the world outside their village. There might not have been any witch burnings for hundreds of years, but the old fears never really died out in small communities like this one. Marianne turned back to the bank of the brook and, collecting her harvest of pussy willow, returned to her classroom to think of a plan. She was concerned that Elsie was isolated and lonely, not necessarily by her own choice. She felt the need to help Elsie become part of the community if she wished.

A few days later Marianne was browsing in the village shop and was attracted by a display of jars and bottles with hand written and illustrated labels which she hadn't seen before.

"What are these?" she asked the shopkeeper, a kindly old man who was a bit deaf but loved helping his wife behind the counter.

"I'm not sure. It's some stuff that Martha took in the other day to sell. What does it say on the label?"

"Wych Hazel, Feverfew, Pellitory, Marsh Marigold. They all seem to be ointments or lotions of some kind. I know Wych Hazel is good for bruises and the children are always falling over or knocking themselves against something so I'll take one of these jars please. The labels are beautiful, somebody is a true artist."

Martha appeared from the back of the shop and said, "They are from Elsie. She has quite an extensive herb garden and has been making these potions and lotions to eke out her income."

"Oh my goodness. I came across her the other day. She seems a gentle lady and lonely I'm sure. She did ask me to call again some time, but I wasn't sure if she really meant it."

Martha handed over the loaded basket with a nod, "The next time she comes in the shop I'll ask her and let you know." Marianne took her purchases and left the shop thinking hard. There had been a case of scarlet fever in the next village school and it was only a matter of time before it reached hers. The disease was a potential killer of children, and even those who survived could have long-lasting side effects. She thought of Elsie's little bottles with their beautiful labels, wondering if there was anything an herbalist could do to help.

A few days later when the school finished for Easter, two of the older boys were leaving, being almost fourteen. Marianne was not sorry to see them go as they were not at all interested in school subjects and were nothing but a distraction to the rest of the single class. But she would miss their almost adult conversations, answering her questions about local matters with witty asides and perceptive takes on local characters. She asked them, "Who is Elsie that lives in The Wee House? What is her family history."

The boys were shocked into silence. Then Charlie muttered, "That's my Auntie Elsie. My Mum goes to see her." With that they ran off, relieved to be done with school for ever.

Marianne enjoyed her Easter break from school. She spent a few days at home with her parents and then came back to the village to tidy up the school classroom and do some research. The scarlet fever epidemic was spreading and several children were absent from the Easter celebrations in church. Marianne resolved to see if she could help at all. She had learned how shy Elsie was and was reluctant to approach her directly so she decided to go and see Charlie's mother and talk to her instead. As they lived in an isolated farm cottage, Marianne pondered the best way to approach the subject. Clearly, to come so far from the road meant she was on a mission so she decided to be as open and honest as possible.

Ellen, Charlie's mother, was busy in her tiny kitchen and was startled to see the teacher on her doorstep. Charlie had left school legally hadn't he? What on earth had he been up to now?

Marianne quickly said, "Please don't worry, this is nothing to do with Charlie. He is a grand boy and you must be proud of him. And his sister Harriet is a joy to teach. I wanted to consult you about a problem that is likely to come soon with all the children."

Ellen invited Marianne into her largely unused parlour and briskly made a pot of tea.

"How can I help you? I've no learning, can't read or write."

"Ah but surely you have a wealth of natural lore? There is a scarlet fever outbreak in the next village and I'm sure it will reach here soon. I'm trying to find someone who can produce remedies to alleviate the symptoms and help the children fight it off. I'm already planning better washing facilities in the school for after the holidays but anything else we can do would be welcome. I understand you are related to Elsie who lives in The Wee House? She seems to have a wealth of knowledge about healing plants?"

Ellen thought for a minute and hesitantly said, "Elsie is my husband's sister. She is very reclusive but I could have a word with her and see what she says."

"That would be wonderful, thank you." Marianne spent the next half hour charming Ellen with tales of schools she had worked in and what a lovely place the village was to live in. She went away hopeful that soon she would be seeing Elsie again.

Two days later, when Marianne was in the village shop, Martha said to her, "Message from Elsie for you," and handed over a sealed note. At home Marianne studied the beautiful flowing hand with pleasure.

'I would be delighted if you could find time to visit me on Saturday afternoon. Please come in the back way, I shall be looking for you. Elsie.'

Saturday was a wonderful sunny afternoon and the meeting was a resounding success. They took tea and home-made biscuits on a little grassy terrace just below the house with the soothing sounds of a small spring which bubbled up through the turf. Elsie proved to be charming.

"I know I look different. I've never really been out of this garden except after dark but my father taught me to read and I've studied the natural world to keep my mind active. You know the little spring here has healing properties. Its reputation goes back in the mists of time but I know it is true, I've used it to help some of the family when they've been ill. It isn't something I want everyone to know, the villagers already think I'm a witch!"

Marianne smiled at her. "You know that before women were called witches, they were Wise-women, and were the local healers and medical practitioners. Their knowledge of herbal remedies was legendary and that knowledge is still around, just gone undercover. Such a shame as with diseases threatening our children, we need every bit of help we can get."

Just then a black cat appeared. It stretched and yawned before sauntering over to Marianne, weaving itself about her legs.

"Oh isn't it friendly. I love cats, especially such glossy black ones as this."

And so saying, she bent down and stroked it lovingly from the top of its head to the end of its tail.

"You must be part 'witch' as well," laughed Elsie. "That cat is very particular about who touches it."

With the cat's obvious approval, the ice was well and truly broken, and Elsie and Marianne became firm friends. Elsie loved having an educated woman to talk to and Marianne was excited at the thought of getting to know this lonely and complex character.

The school opened again after Easter and immediately, Will, Harriet and Jeannie were sent home with sore throats and nasty looking rashes. As Marianne had feared, the scarlet fever epidemic had reached the village but she and Elsie had been busy preparing for it. Using the healing water of the spring, Elsie had made several different syrups; garlic and honey, and apple cider vinegar to soothe sore throats and tongues. She had shown Marianne how to make a balm of Lavender to apply to the rashes and sore skin and they had laid in a store of oatmeal and baking soda for the children to be bathed in. All these were handed out from the school and nobody knew that it was Elsie who had formulated and prepared them until Charlie, not yet used to his drink, let the secret out in the village inn.

Some of the men were all for going to her house and demanding that she stop these 'devilish practices'. Until they went home and told their wives.

"Don't you dare stop her. She is trying her best to save our children and I'm all for it."

Such was the common reaction, and eventually, the wives were proved right.

The epidemic swept through the school and only two children were seriously affected. One, little Will, who was already weakened by cold, hunger and an abusive father, sadly died. Harriet, Charlie's sister, recovered but was left with aching limbs and joints for a lifetime. With Marianne's support, Elsie was seen by the villagers as the saviour of a generation and one or two made the effort to get to know her. They found a warm-hearted, generous soul, friendly and a help to many of the overstressed mothers. The mother of the child who died was emboldened by Elsie's quiet sympathy to rebel against her husband's bullying, and when she answered him back and was beaten for it, he in turn was caught in a back alley and thrashed by some of the outraged men of the village. He was dismissed from his job on the farm and his wife and remaining children were taken in by other families while he was banished from the village.

The school ended for the summer harvest season. Marianne and Elsie had formed a strong bond of friendship over their battle to save the children, and they were enjoying sitting in the tranquil garden, loud with the humming of bees and heavy with the scent of flowers and herbs.

"Will you come and live here with me in The Wee House?"

Marianne was taken aback at Elsie's remark.

"Are you sure? You've always lived on your own, Do you really want someone else in the house?"

"Of course I'm sure. You know how well we get on. Your lodgings are not really comfortable, are they? And I would love the company. To hear all about the children's doings at school would liven my day. Please say yes."

And so Marianne moved into The Wee House and saw for herself how comfortable it was. The little room behind the round dormer was a lovely sunny space for Elsie and Marianne to work writing and illustrating labels. Often, while they worked, a black cat would be sitting outside on the window ledge doing what black cats had always done in that spot. The big downstairs room was cosy with its coal fired range and the two bedrooms under the roof were perfect, one each for the friends. Several years passed in this way and the ladies spent as much time as they could cultivating the garden. Their ambition was to make it a Physic Garden, full of healing plants and herbs, as well as a restful place to work and sit. If Marianne found a promising child, she would ask them into the garden to help and in this way, encouraged the knowledge that gardening and wellbeing went hand in hand. And the children learned to ignore Elsie's strange appearance and enjoy her humour and sympathetic company.

"I've something to ask you Elsie. You know how I value your wisdom and judgement? Well I think I'm in love. I want you to meet him and tell me what you think of him."

"Hmm. I'm not sure I'm qualified. I've never been in love myself. But I would like to meet him."

Amos passed the test and he and Marianne were married and went to live over his parents' grocers shop in the town. As a married woman she was no longer allowed to teach so she frequently visited Elsie. Her concern grew for Elsie's failing health and she would spend the day at The Wee House, preparing remedies, working in the garden and keeping Elsie company. One day she realised Elsie wasn't just sleeping in her chair out in the sun. Her childhood history of rheumatic fever and subsequent heart problems had taken its toll.

To Marianne's surprise, Elsie had left a will leaving The Wee House and all the land associated with it to her, provided she did her best to keep the Physic Garden, and look after the generations of black cats. So Marianne let the house and maintained the garden herself with the aid of children and other helpers.

Thomasina's descendants continued to lord it over The Wee House and its surrounds, and prospective tenants were required to embrace their feline presence.

After Marianne and Amos's second child was born it was obvious that the flat over the shop was too small. "Why don't we move into The Wee House? There is enough room for us if we have an outhouse built for a kitchen and bathroom and the children will have all that lovely space outside to run around in. And a cat to live with."

The move was a great success and the children grew up enjoying the freedom of a large garden with a little spring, lots of beautiful plants and best of all, a tiny room with a round dormer window, often hosting a black cat sunning itself on the window ledge. Although the cats were not overly enamoured of childish play, they learned to accept gentle stroking and taught the children the value of co-operation and respect for animals.

The children, John and Jennifer grew up and left home, but Marianne and Amos continued to live in The Wee House, the place they loved. When Amos died, John inherited the family grocery business, now a chain of three high-class grocers in the county. Jennifer had qualified in Pharmacy, married another Pharmacist and they had built up their company to six businesses in the area. Jennifer loved to visit her mother and see how the healing plants were growing in the garden. When, in 1973, Marianne died, she left the property to Jennifer knowing that she would continue to care for it. And the black cats.

Jennifer was concerned for the future of The Wee House.

"I need to take on a long-term tenant for The Wee House. Someone who likes cats and gardens."

"Yes my dear, that sounds a very good idea." Jennifer's husband, Richard Evans, was supportive of her plan. He liked to pay a visit to The Wee House now and then although he couldn't imagine himself living permanently in a remote village like Garthwaite. He would be happy to have it occupied so the possibility never arose.

In 1999, Richard died, and Evans Chemists was sold. The tenant of The Wee House had recently moved on, and it was ideal timing for the builders to go in and renovate, improve, and decorate. Jennifer was thrilled to be able to move into her old house at the beginning of the new century.

"Hello Jennifer. How are you? What a gorgeous day again. I thought I'd make a start on cutting the grass."

Sam was Charlie's grandson and, like his father, had been a gardener all his life. He had tended The Wee House herb garden as though it was his own whilst the house had been let. The house held a special place in his and his family's hearts and Jennifer, as a skilled herbalist herself, was always happy to gossip with him about the role the Physic garden played in the life of the village.

"Hello Sam, lovely to see you. And yes, the grass is growing and needs attention. It's too much for me to do these days so thank goodness you're willing and able. I plan to weed the lavender bed and get it ready for the season. Our special lavender skin balm sold out quickly last year and I took some cuttings that can be potted on so we can make more this year. You know how I love to use the herbal knowledge my mother passed on to me."

"Yes, and I like helping you. It reminds me of my grandad Charlie's Auntie Elsie. I'm not sure how many of the people who live in the village now know of the wealth of herbal history it contains. Is it because of living here as a child that you went on to study Pharmacy?"

"Yes it was. I love the idea of using plants to heal and by extension, the development of modern medicines. When my husband and I had our chain of Pharmacies, it was always the botanical remedies that attracted me. But the labels were never as beautiful as the ones your grandad's Auntie Elsie painted. You know I have a book inside with examples of them. I'm not sure if they are all there but they look so very attractive."

"Hmmm. That sounds like something that must be preserved. Don't ever let it go will you?"

"Absolutely not. Oh. Here's Tommy. He sleeps more and more these days, I'm wondering if I should let the vet have a look at him."

The black cat came strolling down the grassy slope, his tail not as erect as at one time it would have been and his eyes hooded and misty looking. He rubbed gently against Jennifer's legs and then went to say hello to Sam.

"His coat doesn't look so glossy does it? How old is he now?"

"He must be 18 at least. I had him from the Cat Rescue when I came here 17 years ago and he seemed almost fully grown then. He's a perfect witch's familiar isn't he with his all black coat and green eyes. The latest in a long line of black cats living in this house. If I have to let him go, I'll be sad but will go and find another to keep the succession going. I would have liked to have true descendants of the original cats but I'm afraid diseases saw the line die out. But I'll always have a black cat, vaccinated, neutered and microchipped from the Cat Rescue. The Wee House wouldn't seem like home without one."

## 2019

In 2019 Garthwaite had grown considerably. The nearby railway station made it an ideal commuter village and houses had been built in random patches on the fields. Here seven or eight sizeable villas, there a row of semi-detached houses and, beside the railway line, a couple of dozen small bungalows. A large council housing estate had been tacked on one side and with it a row of shops, a large pub and the doctor's surgery, necessary for such a growing population. A new school had been included in the plans, a welcome addition as the old school was very much in need of repair. The wealthy retirees from the city who bought it on a whim, having seen it on a sunny day with the roses blooming around the door, spent a considerable sum repairing it and making it into the home they had always wanted. Sir Archibald Newbury was a retired civil servant and he and his wife Arabella were fulfilling their lifelong dream to become country dwellers.

The Wee House was still there in the old centre of the village, set back from the road and again almost hidden by large shrubs obscuring the sight of all but the dormers. Even so, there was often a black cat sat on the sill of the small round dormer and the neighbours, who were second homers, had an idea that there was an old lady living there. They had no idea of her family history, or gave a thought to why the cats in the garden were always black.

One day Sam found Jennifer slumped in her chair in tears.

"Look at this letter which came today. I'm in despair."

The letter was from the Council who wanted to buy the land, demolish the house and make an access road through the garden. A few days later Sam found her lying on the floor in pain after a fall. As he called for the ambulance she whispered,

"I don't think I can stay here any longer Sam. Please do all you can to keep The Wee House and herb garden for the village. And I beg you to look after the black cats."

Sam was a man of action and in the pub that night he explained to all and sundry that it would be a shame if The Wee House was demolished and the garden tarmacked over. He remembered his grandfather talking about Auntie Elsie with her striking white streaked hair and birthmark and how she and Marianne had worked so hard to help the children in the scarlet fever epidemic a hundred years ago. Some folk in the village had thought her a witch but her only intention was to offer help to whoever needed it.

"I'll help you." said Mr. Hargreaves, the recently retired lawyer. "I'm used to dealing with councils and know how to put arguments to them."

"We can print off leaflets and distribute them around the village." Roland and Yolande were graphic designers, come to the village to pursue their dream of independence from big business.

And so the offers of help came pouring in. A village meeting was called and a group formed with the aim of buying the house and garden and maintaining them as a community centre and Physic garden. The incomers from the city had all sorts of skills and connections, and this project was just what they wanted to enliven their retirements. Jennifer agreed to donate the property in trust to the group, and in the face of this local opposition, the council backed off. Sir Archibald and Lady Arabella donated a sizeable sum to ensure necessary renovations and alterations, and fund the upkeep.

Whilst Jennifer had gone from the hospital to live in a retirement home, her cat had gone to live with Sam and for the first time in nearly 200 years, there was no resident feline at The Wee House. The local rodent population was left in peace for a while, but only until the neighbouring cats, both tame and feral, discovered the wealth of prey on the plot.

So on January 1st 2020, the Garthwaite Community Interest Group was formed and plans began to be drawn up for the house's new role in the village.

Then in March another epidemic was unstoppably looming and meetings were suspended.

But not the planning.

As soon as it was allowed, groups set to work outside repairing the neglected beds and creating quiet spaces with seats where people could just sit and enjoy the fresh air. And when allowed back inside, the house was redecorated and the downstairs room furnished with comfortable seating to add to the antique furniture left by Jennifer. One upstairs room was shelved out for local archives and the other made into a quiet room for private consultation and therapy. The little room behind the round dormer was retained as a small studio with displays of the original artwork for the labels of Elsie's herbal remedies.

And the outside windowsill was repaired ready for a black cat. A new feline occupant of the honoured position was chosen from the Cat Rescue. As the house was not occupied, Sam and his family took on the role of cat carer, making sure it was fed and kept in good health, but its position as Feline Caretaker of The Wee House was assured.

## 2022

"I think we need to do something to celebrate." Sam was in his usual corner in the village pub, the original one, not the huge modern gastropub out by the council estate. The Garthwaite Arms was centuries old, the one his grandfather had learned to drink in. It was small, dark, cosy and frequented by a core of regulars looking for a music-free place to drink and chat. The only food sold was crisps and pork scratchings.

"Celebrate what?" queried his mate, George.

"Freedom of course. At last we can come out to the pub and meet people inside without wearing those masks and staring at everyone who coughs. Thank goodness for modern medicine. It must have been a nightmare for the folk a hundred years ago."

"Whatever do you mean?" asked another of the regulars.

"The Scarlet Fever epidemic in 1922 of course. Haven't you heard of it? Oh, I suppose not, your family don't come from these parts, do they?"

"Not that far back no. My parents moved here in 1953, the same day as the Queen's coronation. They missed the fun with all the unpacking they had to do. And us kids were small and a bit of a nuisance no doubt. I seem to remember being taken in by a neighbour to watch their little 12 inch black and white telly, but I got bored easily and they soon threw me out again."

"You were always a nuisance Fred. I remember you at school getting up to no good. Ah those were the days." The group sat in silence, contemplating their diminishing pints.

"So tell us about this event in 1922 then. Were you there?" Fred laughed heartily.

"Of course not idiot, I'm two months younger than you and you know it. No, my Grandad Charlie was about 14, just left school and told us kids all about it. His Auntie Elsie was a bit of a witch and she and the teacher made lots of herbal remedies for the children. There wasn't much else in those days. No antibiotics or anything. It must have been a terrible time for the parents worrying if their kids would get it seriously. I know one lad died, there's a memorial in the church in the dark corner by the door to the bell tower. So, I think that as it's just a hundred years since that happened and now we are seeing the back of another epidemic, we should have a celebration. And The Wee House, where Auntie Elsie lived is the place to hold it."

The door opened and a tall, silver-haired gentleman entered, automatically ducking his head.

"Ah, just the chap Reverend. I was telling these incomers here about the memorial plaque in the church to the lad who died of Scarlet Fever in 1922."

"Oh yes, little Will. It was a sad case by all accounts. His father beat him and there was little money in the house for food. He didn't stand a chance really. It's said that the father beat his wife and was duly punished by the village men for it. He disappeared while the wife and other children were taken in by the villagers. The family still has descendants living in one of the council houses. You must know the Kearneys? They've produced some amazing musicians over the years and often play at Barn Dances in the area. Actually, I've been thinking about this very subject. Several of our friends and neighbours in the village have died in this Covid epidemic and we should have a memorial to them. We could combine it with the one for little Will."

The pub regulars thought it was a wonderful idea and, once put to the Wellbeing Centre Trustees, it was not long before a stone mason had been commissioned to produce a new plaque for the church with all the details including little Will. Another was made for the garden of The Wee House. On the day of the festival, the house was decorated with bunting and the garden given extra special attention with tables and chairs set out in the flowery greensward. The schoolchildren had great fun making a decoration for the healing spring in the style of the Derbyshire Well dressings, flower petals stuck onto a clay plaque to form a picture. The whole village was drawn into the party. They had all suffered in various ways in this latest pandemic and it was a most joyous day of relief, friendship and conviviality the photographs of which made a permanent display inside along with Elsie's artwork.

The Wellbeing Centre became a magnet for visitors to the village who enjoyed sitting in the tranquil garden. Inside the house they would go upstairs to look at the beautiful artwork and the photos of the grand celebratory party. They usually made contributions to the care of the resident cat, far more than was needed, and the surplus went to the local Cat Rescue.

To visit Garthwaite you will have to find it first, but once there, you will know The Wee House by the arched dormer window, the peaceful gardens, full of colour and fragrance, sloping down to the river and, most of all, by the glossy black cat, lording it over all from the windowsill.

# Getting Older

I grew a bit more old today,
'Twas such a little sign.
I tried to cut my toe-nails,
To get them all in line.
I managed fine two weeks ago
Just sitting on the bed.
I bent my knee and raised my foot
Towards my inclined head.
The toes were there, all pink and pert
And to my eyes quite clear
And with my clippers in my hand
I cut them without fear.
But now, just sitting on the bed
My knee, it will not bend,
My neck is stiff, my arms too short.
A most alarming trend.
I think I see the toes just there
All stuck onto my feet.
I poke the clippers at 'em. Damn
There's blood upon the sheet.
I'm very cross, I don't feel old
Despite my bus/rail passes.
I cannot get new knees or toes
So I'll go and get new glasses.

## Developments

My toe nails grew again last week,
But now there is a change.
No need to bend and groan and try
To get them all in range.
The effort's much too great for me

I've simply given in.
I know the Anno Domini
Is always going to win.
An advert in the Banner,
Just made me stop and stare.
So I've seen the Foot Health lady
And now I walk on air.

# Revelation

"Oh!" Christine's mouth opened wide in surprise. "This is amazing."

Richard smiled to see her animation. With a voice full of emotion, he whispered, "Hello darling, welcome back."

The relief on both their faces was enjoyed by the watcher. He had seen it so many times before but it never palled.

Christine was a natural chatterbox. Her mother laughed to hear her and encouraged her to chat with the neighbours and friends they met whilst out for their frequent walks around the village.

Her reputation was sealed the day she accompanied her grandparents on their gardening club trip. The club Bore was one of those people who expounded at large on all subjects in a droning monotone. This drove the other members to distraction and the committee had devised a rota of who should sit next to him on the bus to save the sanity of them all. When Christine arrived with her grandparents at the departure point, they didn't realise salvation was at hand. During the outward trip they listened to Christine chattering away to her grandparents and other people, with dawning realisation.

On the return journey, they contrived to sit her in the centre of the back seat, with granny on one side and the Bore on the other.

"Hello dear, did you like the lovely geraniums on the terrace? Weren't they in lovely pots?" He relished the next two hours with an innocent audience.

"They are not geraniums, they are Pelargoniums and unlike geraniums which are frost hardy, the Pelargoniums need to be taken in for the winter. You must dead head them regularly to keep a succession of blooms and they need feeding as well with a Potash rich feed to ensure a good display throughout the summer and winter."

This statement threw him completely. As a confident, eloquent 13-year-old, she had not yet learned to temper her remarks with tact and those overhearing were convulsed with delight.

For the two hour ride home Christine dominated the conversation, the Bore rarely getting in more than a sentence or two before she interrupted to correct him. His discomfiture was complete.

"Can we take her next time?" was the general view.

At school, she was the despair of her teachers as she simply couldn't be quiet and many a lesson was spent in the corridor, especially English and History. Despite this handicap, she passed her O levels with ease and began to enjoy school in the sixth form where discussion was encouraged in preparation for the colleges they were expected to attend.

Inevitably Christine was destined to be a teacher. Talking all day long to a captive audience, what better career?

It was interrupted only a little by marriage and two children. Her mother was delighted to do childcare duties and her husband enjoyed the benefits of the intellectual stimulation that teaching in a prestigious sixth form gave her. He enjoyed listening to her expounding on her day at school and bringing her especially ironic take on the doings of the pupils and staff. And her comments during the television news were worthy of a newspaper column. Richard was a quiet natured man who loved his wife dearly, put up with his colleagues at the insurance offices where he worked and lived for his golf at the weekend.

Richard retired and played a lot more golf. He was naturally, and by training a good listener, enjoying the chat in the bar afterwards and was always interested to hear about Christine's day. So he was concerned when he noticed she was becoming less chatty. There didn't seem to be as much news and comment about her day at school and she was almost silent during news programmes. The only time she showed much animation was when the Prime Minister came on and said, "You must stay at home."

The following day her Head rang up. "We are setting up a platform for remote teaching. I'll let you have all the details soon, we hope to interrupt the student's learning as little as possible in the circumstances."

He was a little surprised at Christine's apparent lack of response but assumed she was as shell-shocked as everyone else at the speed with which life had changed.

Christine didn't really take to the online teaching platform. She found it hard to talk to a screen, struggling to untangle the simultaneous responses from the students. After one particularly difficult day she said to Richard, "I don't think I'm made for this kind of teaching and I'm 59 now so I think I'll retire."

"If you feel it's right for you then go for it."

She finished immediately on the grounds of ill health and officially retired at the end of term.

Weeks passed and Richard noticed how taciturn Christine was. He missed the stimulating conversations they had always had, and her somewhat sideways take on current affairs. They sat through the winter evenings in front of the telly in near silence, Christine often appearing to be asleep as the lack of stimulation led to an inevitable decline in her mental abilities and her consequent depression. Even once the lockdown had been lifted and outdoor meetings were allowed, she was reluctant to go out and meet people. It seemed to Richard that she reached the point where she didn't care about anything. The house took on a neglected air with no fresh flowers and her cooking was definitely not up to scratch. Throughout their long marriage, they had always divided up the chores, Christine doing cooking and laundry, Richard the car maintenance and outdoor jobs. They had a cleaner for the house who of course had gone with the lockdown.

At last, their daughter was able to pay a visit and was shocked at how withdrawn her mother had become.

"Dad, you need to get her to the Doctor. If she's developing dementia it needs to be treated as soon as possible."

Richard managed to arrange a phone call from the surgery and it was a good job he was present as Christine barely responded to the Doctor's questions. It was agreed that a referral to the Geriatrician was urgent and when at last the hospital appointment arrived, Richard happily sacrificed an important golf match to drive her there. The mood in the household was a little lighter although Christine was still uncommunicative. Richard wondered if she would ever be able to talk freely again and reflected on the days when her melodious tones rang constantly through the house. He really didn't look forward to caring for a demented wife. A chatterbox he could deal with but not the morose, unresponsive and occasionally snappy person she had become.

The Geriatrician made his examination and said, "Christine needs to see another specialist. I'll arrange it as soon as possible."

After the second consultation, they had a few weeks to wait before returning to the hospital.

The specialist said, "Shall we do it then? I'll show you first."

"Go on love," encouraged Richard. "You've been waiting long enough, go for it."

Christine smiled at him, not having heard a word, but she did discern the love and concern in his voice and carefully slotted her new hearing aids into her ears.

"Oh!" Christine's mouth opened wide in surprise. "This is amazing."

Richard smiled to see her animation. With a voice full of emotion, he whispered, "Hello darling, welcome back."

## The Winds That Blow

The wind is from the east today, blowing cold and chill.
It wraps its arms about the house and squeezes out the heat.
The droplets in the air take shape as wind and moisture meet
And draws a veil across the land as the haar comes o'er the
hill.

The gale blows from the north today, an arctic, shivering
blast
That stops me in my tracks. I gasp and catch my breath a
while.
As leaves curl up and creatures hide and waves foam in the
Kyle
The wind yields nought, until it's chill moderates at last.

The gentle breeze is from the south, so balmy, soft as down.
Caressing skin and plants alike with warming touch as light
As Mother's kiss. A healing wind that puts all fear to flight.
Awaking smiles and joy alike and banishing all frowns.

The wind that's from the west picks up the moisture from
the sea.
And lets it bathe the land in shades of springtime leafy green.
Releases joy and growth and covers all in freshest sheen.
The west wind's bounteous rain is nature's guarantee.

# NOTE from Barb (Group Leader)

A s a writer, I'm always interested in the ways other writers see the world. So when I heard about Arran's new u3a, I hoped to join a writing group. Instead, I ended up starting one. While most of our members didn't bring publication expertise, it was immediately obvious they had something much more valuable: experience. "Write what you know," writers are told. Well, our group knew a LOT. We brought lifetimes of experiences, memories, and knowledge. We were bursting with stories only we could tell.

As the months passed and we shared, commented, and edited each other's work, I was stunned by their stories told in their voices. Last December, we held a party, and each member of the group received a pin proclaiming them WRITER. This anthology gives a taste of the variety, emotion, and confidence they've achieved.

If you ask them, they'll tell you the truth. "I'm a writer." Truth, like stories, comes in many forms. Here are some of ours.

# Acknowledgements

This book is compiled from the writings of a group of people who are members of the Arran Branch of the u3a. Initially, no-one, except our group moderator, Barb Taub, had written a story which would be published for sale. Barb has, with humour and patience, led us to express our thoughts and memories on paper.

We have learned so much from each other.

Printed in Great Britain
by Amazon

29645772R00069